A GIRL AT WAR

A GIRL AT WAR

GIUSTINA

Lilia Amadio

Translated by
Christopher Ferguson

Originally published in 2010 in Italy by Gruppo Albatros Il Filo Srl, Roma
ISBN 978-88-567-2298-7

Published by
Troubador Publishing Ltd
9 Priory Business Park
Kibworth
Leicester LE8 0RX, UK
Tel: 0116 279 2299
Email: books@troubador.co.uk
Web: www.troubador.co.uk

This is a work of fiction. Any resemblance to events, places, or persons living or dead, is purely coincidental.

ISBN: 9781783064168

Typesetting: Troubador Publishing Ltd, Leicester, UK
Printed and bound in the UK by TJ International, Padstow, Cornwall

Giustina pedalled along cheerfully, humming softly to herself. The white road was full of stones and, so as not to fall, the girl had to try to keep the wheels of her bicycle on one of the two smooth tracks left by the few vehicles that used it.

The road, the Lungomare, ran alongside the beach. It was September of 1938 and the weather was mild, almost an extended summer.

Giustina was happy; eighteen years old, light-hearted and above all happy because she had a boyfriend, Diego, who was showing every sign of being deeply in love with her.

Diego was a good boy; he wasn't from Tortoreto, the village that Giustina came from, in the province of Teramo, but from Giulianova, a fairly large town about five miles away, although in the province of Pescara. Giulianova was known as a port for motorised fishing boats, and Diego worked as a mechanic in a workshop that catered for big-engined motorbikes and bicycles as well as the few motor cars in the area.

Diego was twenty-two years old, and since meeting and falling in love with Giustina Di Giandomenico, he had sorted himself out. He had forgotten the parties and dances that he used to frequent on a Sunday so he could devote himself entirely to his young girlfriend. He had met her by chance, at a party at a friend's house, and since then, he had thought only of her. She was a good-looking girl, young and full of life, a little taller than average, her head was covered by light-brown curls and she had blue eyes. There was something special about her; a kind of passion contained by good manners, and a way of moving and walking that was almost feline. She, without trying, attracted all kinds of attention. Her parents ran a little shop in Tortoreto in which you could find anything, from pasta to stamps, from salt to linen.

Giustina was an only child, and her parents were not young. She was born when Natalina, her mother, was already forty and her father, Donato, was forty-five. The baby was welcomed as a precious gift and there was nothing that they were not ready to do for her.

When Giustina first told them that she was in love with a young mechanic from Giulianova, they were worried. However, when they made enquiries, they found the only blemish on his character was his taste for racing, which he did on the rare occasions he could persuade his boss to lend him his old Harley-Davidson for a few hours.

Apart from that, Diego Moretti was a serious young man who was worthy of respect.

Giustina seemed very much in love, and her mother was quick to put her on her guard: "You're still a child, don't give in to your boyfriend when he pressures you. Be careful! Men are always the same, always asking for an advance on the wedding night!"

"It's all right, mother," Giustina replied serenely, "Diego is different; he loves and respects me. And he wants to marry me, as soon as he can."

Giustina said nothing about how Diego's ardent caresses upset her, and the insistent impulse he had to squeeze her in his arms so that she could feel the impetuosity of his desire against her belly.

Giustina pedalled happily, smiling, thinking about Diego. The evening before, he had kissed her for a long time behind the wall of the house in the dark. He had passionately caressed her firm breasts.

"Will I be able to resist for a year?" the girl asked herself. "I'll have to be more careful."

She arrived at the shop and leaned her bicycle against the wall, close to the door. Her mother was serving a customer, weighing charcoal for her. Giustina moved towards her silently. When the customer had left, she examined the pieces of fabric that were placed one on top of the other. There was one in particular that had been attracting her attention since its delivery a few weeks ago. It was light blue with pink flowers and little green leaves. What a dress she could make with that fabric! She was good with a needle, and her friends envied her her "golden hands".

Natalina saw Giustina's gaze and smiled. "We're not rich enough to use the shop's stock for ourselves," she said with tenderness, "but, seeing as you like it so much, we can make an exception with that fabric. I just have to remind you that the summer has gone: what are you going to do with a cotton dress?"

"It's not for right now, mother, but for my honeymoon. A year passes quickly."

"I keep forgetting that we'll lose you in a year, my little one."

"You won't lose me, mamma, I'll always love you!" Giustina embraced her mother.

Giustina wondered what really would happen to the shop after she was married. Her parents were now rather advanced in years and without her would struggle to keep it going. It was she who opened the shop early in the morning, she who took the deliveries and checked them, she who kept the accounts.

If she and Diego found a house in Tortoreto, she could continue to help her parents after she was married, at least until children arrived. However, Diego wanted to put down his roots in Giulianova to be near to his garage. He cared about his work. He was skilful, precise and meticulous, and his boss, Antonio Capuani, greatly appreciated him. For this reason, living away from Giulianova seemed out of the question. It would be difficult for him to travel every day by bicycle to work, if he went along with Giustina's wishes, especially in winter.

That afternoon, Giustina got herself ready with a lot of care. She knew that Diego would be there any moment to take her out and she wanted to look beautiful; it was Sunday, and they both deserved a relaxing day after a week of hard work.

When Diego arrived with his boss's motorbike, the one with the sidecar, she smiled happily. She kissed him quickly on the cheek and asked him:

"How did you get Mr Capuani to lend you the sidecar? He loves it."

"I worked like a black so that he couldn't say no; he knows I'm crazy about this bike. Get in, I'll take you for a ride, so that the whole village can admire you."

She got carefully into the sidecar. She tied a handkerchief under her chin, and turning to Diego, said, "I'm ready! Let's go!"

Diego set off, pushing the accelerator down. He rode quickly and laughed happily when people waved at them in recognition. Giustina was proud of him: no one else she knew could ride a motorbike at all, let alone as well as Diego could.

Diego passed the level crossing and set off with speed towards Giulianova along the Nazionale. The trees flanking the road flew past them and the wind ruffled their hair.

Giustina looked at her man. He was concentrating hard on the road, with a serious and intense expression. He was handsome, with dark curls that blew in the wind. He realised that she was watching him and asked: "Why are you looking at me, darling? Are you frightened?"

"I'm looking at you because you're beautiful and I love you very much."

His reaction was to steer off the road to the right, down a little road that became a track in the fields.

"Where are you taking me?" she asked, worried.

"Into the countryside! I want to hold you and kiss you for a while."

They continued on for about a kilometre and found themselves in endless fields; there were no houses nearby, but there were several big bales of hay piled up.

Diego stopped the bike and took the girl by the hand, pulling her between two tall bales. He pulled her close and began to kiss her lips and neck. Giustina tried a little weak resistance.

He unbuttoned her dress and put his hands on her breasts.

"I want to look at you, darling, don't say no."

She let him continue, sensing his desire. Diego took her breasts in his hands. They were big, ripe, beautiful. He sucked on them, then took her hands and pressed them on his belly.

"What are you doing? What do you want?" Giustina asked, confused.

"Wait, darling, wait. Let me…"

He held her tight against him and moved slowly, holding her around her waist and kissing her almost violently. She offered no resistance, because she liked the way Diego had with her and she felt an uncontrollable desire to give in to him. She moved herself along with him until he stopped.

He broke loose from her and looked at her lovingly.

"I'm sorry, I just love you so much."

When they got back to the bike they seemed shy of each other.

Diego couldn't find the heart to speak because he knew he hadn't behaved in a way that Giustina's parents would have approved of, had they known. Furthermore, the girl was underage.

Giustina was also silent. She had felt a marvellous sensation of complete abandonment with Diego up against her. At the same time, she realised that, if she indulged him, they would never reach their wedding day without some mess or other.

Diego broke the silence, slowing down as they reached Tortoreto.

"Darling, I'm sorry. I shouldn't behave like that with you; you're my fiancée. It's just that you're so beautiful... I love you so much. I'll try to hold off until we're married, I promise."

He took her hand. On her finger was the little engagement ring he had struggled to buy her: a thin circle of gold with a tiny aquamarine. He held it tightly while he rode along slowly, then held it to his lips.

He stopped in front of the house and Giustina got out.

"Won't you come in?" she asked him.

"I don't think I should. I feel guilty."

"Don't be silly. Nothing happened, really, did it?"

He looked at her. Her round, smiling face, her cheeks reddened by the ride, her shining blue eyes; his little underage fiancée was also wiser than him.

Still he decided not to follow her in.

They had found, and – with great difficulty – bought, a little house on the outskirts of Giulianova, a little back from the Nazionale, in the middle of the countryside. It boasted a large kitchen with a fireplace, a bedroom and a bathroom. There was even another tiny little room, complete with a window. Giustina could keep her sewing machine and the bicycles there until a baby arrived. There was a day bed as well, ready for any eventuality.

There was a fenced garden around the house in which stood a fine pine tree, surrounded by oleanders. Behind the house were a vegetable patch and a well; there would also be space, one day, for a few chickens. The back door gave onto the garden through the back wall of the kitchen. On one side of the garden, a large mimosa grew.

Giustina had put a lot of time into decorating the house, aided by her mother. The bedroom furnishings were a gift from her parents: they were gorgeous, of solid carved walnut. The window was decorated with lace curtains she had crocheted herself.

The kitchen was also very welcoming. It had a big, beautiful glass-fronted cupboard that showed off the coffee cups – wedding gifts – beside the wine glasses. Red gingham curtains hung at the window and on the French door onto the garden. In the centre of the room sat a marble-topped table, circled by straw-backed chairs.

Diego was proud of the house. They weren't rich, but with his job he could provide his family with dignity and comfort.

The wedding was drawing near, and there were lots of things to be done.

With the big day in mind, Giustina's parents were negotiating the sale of their shop to a neighbour. They wouldn't be able to keep going without her help, and, although they were sorry for it, they didn't want Giustina to suffer for them. They had helped the young couple to buy the house and, with the rest of their savings, could afford to live frugally the rest of their lives.

"If things go along as they are now," said Donato, Giustina's father, "we'll be all right. But if war breaks out…"

When he spoke like this, his wife always stopped him.

"You're always thinking the worst! There won't be a war."

It was the end of the summer, 1939, and the situation in Europe was tense and unstable.

"A few years ago I was fighting Germans in the Great War, now we've signed a pact with Berlin! Who knows what will happen?"

Diego would sometimes talk with him. He took no interest in politics; he never went to the rallies. This was perhaps because, living in the countryside, things that went on in Rome – or in Europe – seemed very far away. The little information he got came, like it did for everyone, from gossip at the bar, from the radio or from the LUCE films and documentaries he saw at the cinema with Giustina. Back home, he had two much-older spinster sisters and his mother. They never spoke about politics.

"If there's a war," Donato told him, "You'll be the first to go. You're young, they'll call you up and send you who-knows-where."

"Papà!" cried Giustina. "We're getting married in a few days! Don't go saying these things!"

Donato said nothing more, but shook his head.

Giustina and Diego were married on the 1st of September that year. The same day the Nazis invaded Poland.

They didn't go far for their honeymoon. A well-off aunt of Giustina's had given them the use of a little villa near Pescara where they could spend a couple of quiet weeks. Giustina had dreamed of a honeymoon in Rome, a place she had never visited, although she was now almost twenty. Money was short, however, and she didn't want her parents spending the savings they needed to live on, now that they had sold the shop. They left Pescara earlier than they had planned because of the worrying news on the radio: on the 3rd of September, Britain and France had declared war on Germany. Italy was not yet involved, but how long would that last?

Despite these worries, Giustina was happy: these were the best days of her life. She kept the house clean, cooked, and tended the garden. She even planted flowers because she wanted the garden to be welcoming and full of colour. Diego would come home in the evening, after closing the garage. When he could, he even brought his wife a little present – a flower, a bead necklace, a cake.

He would come into the house and run straight to her. He was exuberant, he wanted to make love to her and wouldn't take no for an answer. But being with him was wonderful for Giustina as well; she waited anxiously on his return because she felt a boundless love for him. In the last months of their engagement, it was hard for her not to give in to him. Diego loved and wanted her; as much as he tried to control himself, as he had promised, he couldn't keep his hands to himself. It was his way of communicating with her.

He was a man of few words. He could only talk about cars and motorbikes; all the rest he said with gestures and actions.

He sought her out without speaking; he kissed her and made her feel how much he desired her. Giustina took him in her arms and let him do as he wished, because making love to him was beautiful. She had waited for that moment as if all her busying about the house all day was for just one reason: feeling, in Diego's arms, that absolute sense of ecstatic breaching that made her so happy. Diego was never satisfied; his young wife attracted him in a way that dizzied him. Often, he would wake in the night to hold her and make love to her again.

At Christmastime, Giustina found that she was pregnant. Diego was proud and happy and Giustina's parents were also unable to hide their delight.

The baby was to be born in August. In March, Diego's conscription card arrived. The situation in Europe had got worse and Italy was to go to war alongside Germany.

Giustina cried in Diego's arms.

"How can they call you up? You're married and I'm pregnant. Can't you do something?"

Diego held her close and told her: "Don't be afraid. They're calling me up to finish the training I had during National Service. We're not at war yet."

"But you'll lose your job. Your boss won't wait; he'll hire someone else."

"I'll send you all my pay, Giustina, what little I get. I'll try and make Corporal, and then we'll be ok. But, Giustina, if my country calls, what else can I do?"

Giustina fell silent. She remembered her father talking about the war and fascism. She didn't understand politics, but it seemed absurd that someone, a father of a family, could be snatched from his wife and sent off to a distant land just because someone ordered it. She felt powerless, and at that moment the desire to understand grew in her, the desire to go deeper into the real problems of politics and war. Diego set off for Rome and when he came back for a few days a month later, he seemed changed. To Giustina, he looked taller and stronger, with his hair cut short and a steady gaze.

Her love for him was enormous. She had him take her in his arms over and over again in those few days they had together. Deep in her heart, she feared that their little piece of happiness was in danger of disappearing. She was entering her fifth month. After Diego left, she decided to stay with her parents, at least until the baby was born. She was often seized by sudden fears and unknown terrors: if she were to feel ill at night, who could help her? Who could she have called, in that lonely place?

Diego wrote often from Rome. Giustina read his letters with a smile. They had both only attended the *liceo tecnico* up to third year, but she had learned more than him, perhaps as a result of the business correspondence and the bookkeeping she had done for her parents. So she was aware of Diego's occasional spelling mistakes. How he wrote was not, however, important to her; she kissed the page where he had signed his name, tears in her eyes. She missed him and the tenderness he had brought to their lovemaking in those few months of married life.

She always replied to his letters straight away. She tried to fill them with all the little details of her day and especially the kicks that their baby gave her: constantly in motion, it seemed the child could not wait to be born. In March, Diego wrote that he was being transferred to southern Italy for training, and that he was following the course to be made corporal successfully. He was appreciated, respected and treated well by everyone. Giustina came to know through friends that Diego's boss had hired another mechanic, Attilio Di Mizio. Giustina knew him because he had been a friend of Diego's. She didn't write to tell him this because she did not want to up set him, and the chances were that Attilio would also be called up and have to leave the garage before long.

Often, using whatever transport she could, she would head to Giulianova to check the house, to water the garden and do some weeding. She would also go round to the garage to see what was new. The boss knew that Attilio could get called up any day, and was worried about finding a suitable replacement for him.

"If you find yourself short", Giustina told him, "I'll come and give you a hand, if only with the bicycles." Antonio Capuani was a good-looking man of about fifty. He was a widower and had no children.

"If only!" he replied. "First, get this baby into the world and then we'll do something, you and I." Saying this, he winked at Giustina; such a pretty girl with those big blue eyes and that unknowingly suggestive body. With her husband away, he thought, she must be in need of some kind of comfort.

On the 10th of June, Italy entered the war as Germany's ally, attacking France. A few days before, Diego and his regiment had departed for the French front. They attacked on the 21st of June and in three days the war, on that front at least, was won. France had surrendered and Italy could consider herself conqueror of a country that had already, in fact, been defeated by the Germans. Diego, who had worried about how unprepared the Italian military had seemed, was writing strange letters that Giustina found hard to interpret. She knew censors made it difficult for servicemen to express views against the regime or dissatisfaction with the war effort, but he transmitted through the news he sent her a deep sense of unease. Furthermore, it was getting cold, and Diego, who was probably on the border, was complaining about it: there had been cases of frostbite among the troops.

In August, Giustina gave birth to Gabriele, a bouncing baby boy. In looks, he took after his mother, with his blue eyes and wavy hair. Diego wasn't there: he was in a military hospital in France with pneumonia, and had been for several weeks. Giustina knew his condition must be serious because he hadn't written often and when he did, the letters were short and contained little detail about his health. In October, he came home on sick leave. He hadn't told Giustina of his return, and the shock of it almost floored her. He was different. He looked pale, thin and worn down. But he was happy to finally meet his child, who looked, he said, even more beautiful in real life than he was in the photos his wife had sent him.

Giustina wanted to go back to their house, with Gabriele and Diego, at least until the end of his sick leave. He was still sick; he had a persistent cough that no medicine was helping. She was making a real effort to curb her desire for him: he had been away a long time, and she loved him a great deal. But she did it, out of fear for his health.

"You know what I would like, Diego? I'd like to get pregnant again, so that when you come home from the war, there will be another baby for you. That will keep me busy while you're away."

Diego smiled sadly.

"The war has only just started. Who knows how long it will last? If I go along with this, and we make a baby every time I'm on leave, we might end up with family that we can't afford to feed."

She pulled him close and covered his face with kisses. He had changed from the boy she had married. Now he was quieter, more serious, and less effusively amorous than before, perhaps because of his illness. His curly hair was now straight and short, and his face, while still young, was careworn.

Giustina vowed to nurse him back to health as best she could. Although it was already getting difficult to find rationed foodstuffs, she managed to feed him healthy food: meat, eggs and fresh vegetables.

Slowly, Diego's health returned. His cough was gone, and a glow had come back into his cheeks. He felt strong again, and made love to Giustina with the passion of the first months of their marriage. She was happy and couldn't bear to think of his leave coming to an end. He had to go to Rome for a check-up and when the time came to leave, Giustina and Gabriele went with him to the station. She held him for a long time. "Write to me straight away, and tell me everything. Don't keep me waiting."

"Don't worry. I feel much better. And … and I love you."

He looked around him and kissed her quickly on the mouth. They were husband and wife, certainly. But the village was still a village.

After a few days, Diego's letter arrived. He had passed his inspection, he was completely over the pneumonia, and could enter back into service. However, now he was to be posted to Campania. Giustina was disappointed. She had hoped his sick leave would be extended. She hadn't managed to get pregnant and had no idea when she would next see him.

She followed news of the war on the radio and found herself often wanting to discuss it with her father. She had come back home to her parents, occasionally travelling to the house in Giulianova by bicycle. There she could see tangible signs of Diego's presence: his blue jumper over the chair, his striped pyjamas under the pillow, a pack of his cigarettes that he left behind because he was stopping smoking for a while. There were even a few French matches he had brought back from the front. "If only I were pregnant," she thought, "I would have something of Diego inside of me." She looked in the mirror, and was struck by how bright her eyes looked. She realised then all she needed was for Diego to be close to her.

In October 1940, Italy attacked Greece. Giustina was worried that Diego might be sent to the front line, despite his recent recovery. He was an infantryman, and she understood that the infantry were always the first to go. However, Diego remained in Italy for the moment and people were starting to talk about sending forces to northern Africa in support of the troops stationed in Italy's colonies there. The news from that front had begun to get more and more worrying for Italy.

In the middle of September, Marshall Rodolfo Graziani had penetrated seventy kilometres into Egyptian territory and had reached the town of Sidi Barrani. However, by the end of the year, the British had counterattacked and forced the Italians back to Bardi, Tobruk and finally, by February 1941, to Bengasi, and they lost control of the whole of Cyrenaica. Since so many Italians had been killed and taken prisoner, Italy had no choice but to send more troops, only this time under German command.

Diego was sent to Cyrenaica just as Rommel's Afrika Korps were pushing the British back on the way to re-conquering the region. Giustina was resigned. She was living on fear and the little official news she got from the radio and the newspapers. She sought news from her father and cried in her mother's arms.

Diego wrote to her, but his letters were light on detail. He was well, but the climate was horrible: extremely hot during the day and freezing cold at night. In his letters, despite the reserve that had always characterised his relationship with her, he spoke of loving her, of missing her, of thinking about his child. It was a kind of wistful homesickness that struck Giustina to the core. She wept at their misfortunes: what kind of a married life was this?

Her father, who secretly listened to Radio London, had told her that the British were preparing a counterattack. She would wake up in the middle of the night, covered in sweat and could not get back to sleep.

"They say it's up to the men to fight," she complained to her mother, "but am I not fighting my own war as well? My husband has been taken away, my baby has no father, I have nothing to live on, and if it weren't for you, we'd be dead from hunger already." And bitter tears ran down her face.

The situation in North Africa was fluid. The British had attacked in November 1941 and pushed the Italian and German forces out of Cyrenaica as far as borders of Tripolitania. Then, in May of 1942, the Germans were able to retake Tobruk, from where they were able to move on to and past the Egyptian frontier, coming to a halt at El Alamein, thanks in part to the supplies captured from the British. It was June of 1942 and there had been little news from Diego. Giustina tried to follow the fortunes of the war with help from her father and her old geography textbooks from school. She followed Diego's progress on the maps, trying to imagine what it must be like, going backwards and forwards across Cyrenaica.

The telegram from the Military Command caught her unprepared. Diego was back in Italy. He had fallen sick again and was in a hospital at Torre Annunziata, near Naples.

She borrowed the money she needed from her parents and set off with one of Diego's sister, Silvana. Silvana was thirty-six and had a position of responsibility in a packing factory in the village. Giustina could count on her resourcefulness on the long journey through places she had never been. They had to get to Rome first and then take the first train they could to Naples from Termini station. Giustina, who had dreamed of visiting Rome on her honeymoon, saw only the railway station of the Eternal City, where they stopped just long enough to work out the right platform for the Naples train.

Their journey was long and arduous, spent crowded into bulging compartments reeking of smoke. Silvana was pensive and silent; Giustina could barely look at her, her stomach heaving with anxiety. She was thinking about Diego: if he had been sent home from North Africa, it must either be a serious illness that was untreatable in the field, or a war wound.

The two exhausted women reached Torre Annunziata in the early afternoon on the day after they had set out. Before being admitted to the ward where Diego lay, the medical officer, Captain Mancini, wanted to speak to Giustina.

"Ma'am, your husband was sent back from El Alamein seven days ago. He has tuberculosis, and I have to say it looks pretty bad. As you know, there's no specific medicine he can take or cure to follow: he needs good food, mountain air and rest. All things in rather short supply in wartime, I'm afraid. I'll take you to see him now. He's rather fed up, and won't stop thinking about you and his boy. But please remember that he's sick, ma'am, and that his sickness is contagious. Be careful!"

Like a robot, Giustina thanked the captain and followed the soldier who led her to her husband, holding on to her sister-in-law's arm. They came into a small ward that held just six beds. Diego was by the window, lying on his side at the far end of the room. Giustina ran to him, holding her arms wide. Diego, her cheerful, outspoken Diego, always so sure of himself, was prostrated on the bed, his head shaved, his face sickly and pale beneath his unnatural colouring. His body was thin and his bones stretched his skin. He took her hand and his eyes filled with tears.

"You came. I've been waiting to see you. I'm not well, Giustina, but I will be soon. I can recover. Thanks, Silvana, for looking after my wife for me. You've come so far."

Every word required an effort.

Giustina sought to reassure him. "I'm sure you'll be fine, darling. Don't you think so, Silvana?

"Now, don't speak, it's not good for you. Let me talk to you. Gabriele is doing very well and sends you a kiss. I am so happy to see you. You ought not to worry, they'll make you better and soon I'll be able to take you home."

She felt like she was lying. Suddenly, Diego began to cough. He put a handkerchief to his mouth and the two women saw it become covered with blood. Giustina could not control herself: she burst into tears. Silvana put her hands on her shoulders and spoke to her brother.

"You have to get well, Diego. Mr Antonio is waiting for you at the garage. He can't find anyone as good a mechanic as you. Give it all you've got, you've just got to see how beautiful little Gabriele is."

Diego smiled. His smile, hesitant and shy, was very different from the grin that had captured Giustina's heart. He seemed to be ashamed of being ill.

"I'm becoming a burden, Giustina. The war's only been going two years and I've had two serious illnesses. What are you going to do with me?"

"Just think of getting better, my love. The only thing that matters to me is that I get you home. If you can't work, I'll work for you."

"What was that you called me? 'My love?' You've never called me that before."

Giustina blushed. She had never used those words before, words that seemed to belong to an actress in the movies, a *femme fatale*. Diego had called her his love before, when they were courting and his passion was in full flow.

Diego started coughing again, and again blood spread over the handkerchief. The sisters-in-law looked at each other as the severity of his illness began to dawn on them.

"We'll stay in Torre Annunziata for a few days to be with you. Then we'll come back down again later on."

Giustina took her husband's hand between her own.

"You're looking well, Giustina. Being away from me does you good."

Diego's voice was fading.

"I've been living on my nerves and little else since you've been gone, Diego. I feel much worse without you."

It was the first time she had ever spoken to him like this, in front of someone else. She was unashamed.

"Staying here costs money, Giustina, and we have very little of that. I've lost my combat bonus because I'm here in hospital. How will we get by? And if I don't get better, what will we live on? We will have to depend on your parents, and they don't have a lot. And my folks can hardly help us: they have nothing. And there's my mamma and sisters... Poor Silvana here, who should be getting married..."

Diego seemed to be panicking. He could not look his wife in the eye.

"Don't worry about these things, Diego. You have to concentrate on getting better. We can deal with the rest later."

They had to leave him then, so as not to tire him out. In the corridor just outside the ward, the two women embraced tearfully. Giustina was sobbing. "He's so sick. How can he recover from this? It's the sort of thing that kills you."

Silvana could not find the strength to speak. Diego, being ten years her junior, was almost like a son to her and her sister. She knew that only a miracle could save him. Giustina was right.

They came back to visit him in the following days. They had taken a room with a fisherman's family and tried to spend as little as they could on food. Diego's condition was stable, but his morale worsened with each passing day. It seemed that only now was he beginning to realise how dangerous the situation was. The only cures for his illness would be expensive and, even then, uncertain. How could he manage? Where would they find the money? Overcome with depression, he revealed the depths of his anxiety to his wife.

"If I get a bit better but remain sick in the long run, I have no idea how I'll make enough money to feed you and Gabriele. On the other hand, should I die, you'll get a war pension and be able to live comfortably enough."

"You will get better, Diego. You're young; everything will be back as it was. If you can't earn enough, I'll help out. I'm strong and willing."

"That's not what we planned. When we married… we didn't imagine… that I … that I would be so useless."

In the evenings, Giustina would talk with Silvana, who seemed less and less hopeful that Diego would be able to recover. "There is no cure for it," she said, shaking her head, "and there is nothing we can do but wait and hope. Now, however, we have to go home. I have to go back to work. We'll try and come back down as soon as I can get away again."

The two women went back to the hospital the morning before they were to return to Giulianova. At the entrance the guard stopped them: Captain Mancini wanted to see them. Giustina turned to Silvana, shaking. "Do you think he's got worse?"

Mancini was waiting for them with a look of tremendous grief on his face as they came in. They spoke in unison. "What's happened? Why can't we see Diego?"

He took Giustina's hand and held it between his own. "Ma'am, I don't know how it happened. He was so desperate. He had lost all will to live… you yourself must have realised that…"

"What do you mean? What's happened to my husband?" Her voice shook with the sobs she was struggling to hold back.

"Ma'am… Diego has put an end to his life."

"No! No!" Her voice was barely human. She ran towards Diego's ward, followed by her sister-in-law, before the Captain could stop them.

Reaching the ward, she ran towards her husband's bed. He was still lying there, lifeless, his face calm, a small pink hole in his right temple. His pistol was in his hand. The tragedy must have happened just a short time ago.

Giustina could not bear the sight: she fell to the ground, unconscious. Silvana covered her face with her hands and sobbed in desperation. Two soldiers lifted Giustina on to a chair while someone ran to fetch her a glass of water. When she came round, she confronted the Captain.

"How could you leave a pistol with a desperate man who has an incurable disease? How could you? Did no one see him? Did no one try to stop him?"

She was now sobbing uncontrollably. She moved towards Diego and saw that his little pink wound was crawling with lice. She fled, followed by Silvana who was worried what she might do in a moment of desperation.

"My God! Like a dog... they wouldn't let a dog die like this!"

She could not accept the injustice of such a death. Only twenty-seven! And they had been married such a short time!

Captain Mancini took her gently by the shoulders and guided her back into his room. He offered her a seat, saying, "Ma'am, Diego realised he was gravely ill. He knew that he could be sick for a number of years, leaving his family in complete poverty. That was what worried him most. He made the choice to end his life for you and your son and your financial well-being. He realised he was not going to make it, and I believe the illness would have claimed him in due course."

Seeing Giustina still dazed, he handed her a note. She recognised Diego's handwriting and florid signature.

'I fought for my country, I fell ill in the service of my country. I die so that my wife and child might receive the war pension due to them at my death.'

It took Giustina an infinity to read those lines through her tears.

"Ma'am, I give you my word of honour that I will do everything in my power to see that you get that pension as soon as possible. I will make every effort for the memory of Diego. I was very fond of him, you see. We met in France at the start of the war."

Giustina and Silvana lived the days that followed in a trance. They buried Diego there in Torre Annunziata, far from home and travelled back in grief, alone, because there was no money to bring his body back to Abruzzo.

When she came back home, to her parents and Gabriele, Giustina closed herself up in a silence that frightened everyone around her. She was ill, would not see anyone, would not answer questions, would not eat. No one must know that Diego had killed himself: that point she agreed with Silvana.

Natalina, Giustina's mother, would bring Gabriele to her room because only with him did she seem to be alive at all. She caressed him in silence, and held him as she cried. Natalina even thought of going to the parish priest for help. Surely he could persuade Giustina to accept the tragedy. He knew the young woman well; she had received First Communion and Confirmation in his parish. Giustina refused to meet him without explaining why. She would never forget the pain caused by the military chaplain's refusal to bless Diego's body back in Torre Annunziata because he had taken his own life. The lack of pity shown by the priest and by the Church towards a poor, sick, young man was inexcusable, incomprehensible. Her parents would just have to wait for her pain to ease, no matter how long it took. For the time being, Giustina seemed to have lost all interest in life. She had no hope, no will to go on living.

Just before Christmas, however, she suddenly decided to go back to the house in Giulianova, leaving Gabriele with his grandparents. She was twenty-three years old now, and couldn't accept being kept by her mother and father. The war pension, even with Captain Mancini chasing it up, would take some time to come through and in the meantime she would have to find work. In the meantime, and perhaps even afterwards, because the amount she was to receive made her cry in desperation, knowing that such a pitiful sum could hardly afford her child a happy and carefree life. That said, these were difficult times and there was not much work around.

The best opportunities were to be found in the countryside because all the able-bodied men had been called up into the army. She found the job she was looking for at a farm a few miles outside the town. She picked fruit and vegetables, sowed seed in the ploughed fields and oversaw the irrigation systems. It was hard work and she needed to be out in the fields from dawn to dusk, but she never complained. She had had a far easier life with her parents, but having made the decision to work, she made every sacrifice necessary, knowing that it would help Gabriele.

Sometimes, when she passed by on her bicycle, she stopped at Diego's old garage to say hello. Attilio had been called up as well, and Antonio now had only a rather shambling old mechanic to help him. When Antonio saw her, he came up to her with a smile on his face and a look in his eyes that was a little forward, a touch insolent.

"Hello! Is that you coming home from work? You look tired. Come, I've some fruit for you. Would you like a beer?"

"Thanks for the fruit, Mr Antonio, but I don't drink beer."

"Listen, if you want, someday you could come over for dinner? I'm on my own, you know, and I'd like your company." As he spoke, he stroked her arm, squeezing her sensually.

Giustina did not pull away. Nothing really mattered to her. If he wanted to, let him stroke her arm. She would take the fruit for Gabriele.

But she never accepted the offer of dinner, and came less and less often to the garage.

The months passed, each the same as the last. She worked in the fields and rode to Tortoreto whenever she could to see Gabriele and bring him whatever she had managed to scrape together through the week.

The tide of the war, which up to the end of 1941 had seemed in favour of Germany – and therefore Italy – was beginning to turn. The Japanese attack on Pearl Harbour in December of that year had seen the Americans enter the war. American forces arrived in North Africa alongside the British and had the measure of the Italians and Germans within a few months. Between the 9th and 10th of July 1943 the Allies landed in Sicily, plunging Italy into crisis. Mussolini's government fell on the 25th and the king appointed Marshall Badoglio to form a new government. The Germans, long concerned about the inadequacies of their ally, put into action their contingency plans to occupy Italy in the event of her exit from the war. On the 8th of September, Italy surrendered to the Anglo-American Allies and Germany began her occupation of Italian territory. Following the invasion of Sicily, the Allies had landed in Calabria and Salerno in early September. Badoglio, his government and the King fled Rome for Bari.

Despite these important events that were disrupting the life of the nation, Giustina's life changed little. A German command post had been set up in Giulianova's police headquarters and some locals, nostalgic for the former regime, were collaborating with the occupiers. There was much suspicion between people, a growing fear that no one could be trusted, even those previously thought of as friends.

In the days following the 8th of September, Giustina met Attilio, who had returned home after the disintegration of the Italian armed forces in the German occupied territories. They met by chance, one evening on a side street. All the young men were staying hidden, knowing that the Germans would send them off to work in the war effort if they were found. She was amazed to see him and greeted him warmly, knowing that she would be able to talk about Diego with him, even if she could never mention the truth about his death. Attilio thought like everyone else that Diego had died of tuberculosis in hospital. He told her that he didn't always sleep at home because he was scared of the

Germans raiding the house and finding him. Instead he slept here and there, at farmhouses or in haystacks in the countryside.

Giustina found out from her father that a number of officers from the disbanded Italian army had refused to recognise the fledgling Fascist Republic of Salò and were planning to carry out acts of sabotage against the German forces in the area.

"Isn't that dangerous?" she asked. "What will happen if someone spills the beans on them?"

"They'll be arrested and either shot or taken to Germany as forced labour. That's what will happen."

"But that's terrible! They are only defending their country. Aren't they prisoners of war?"

"You think the Germans care about stuff like that? They are a cruel people, Giustina, that's what I've always said. Look what happens when you ally yourself with people like that!"

One evening, Giustina was seated at the table, her elbows bent and her face in her hands. She was deeply sad: it was her wedding anniversary. She saw with her mind's eye her husband's fevered eyes that seemed to ask for forgiveness and then, above all else, the image of him stretched out on his bed, a pink wound in his temple.

The war pension had arrived. Captain Mancini, so fond of Diego, had kept his promise. The widow and orphan of his best NCO would not go without. Gabriele was still back in Tortoreto with his grandparents. The pension alone was not enough for both her and her son. Since the Italian surrender and the German occupation, there was almost nothing to buy outside the black market. She hoped that, through working in the fields where there was still a lack of men, she could scrape together something for Gabriele: eggs, potatoes or fresh vegetables.

It was the end of November 1943 and the winter promised to be a harsh one; perhaps there would even be snow.

"It never rains but it pours," she thought sadly.

She was cold; she had little wood for the fire and was trying hard to save what she had. Over her black woollen stockings she had pulled a pair of socks that she had stitched together out of scraps from an old shirt belonging to her mother. She had her father's old wool coat over her dress. Her frozen hands were pulled into the long sleeves as she tried to warm them.

When she heard the knock at the door, she jumped up and went over cautiously.

"Who is it?" she inquired, after a moment's hesitation.

"Please open the door, Giustina. It's me, Attilio."

"What do you want at this hour?"

"Just open the door, please."

Giustina opened the door and Attilio came in. He was behaving strangely, suspiciously.

"What's happened?" she asked apprehensively.

"Nothing too unusual. I need your help. I need to hide someone for a fortnight, a partisan. You know that where I live in town he'll been seen straight away. Here, you're far enough away that no one will notice."

"You're crazy, Attilio. How can I take in a stranger for a fortnight? I'm on my own here, and what you're asking me to do is dangerous. Why should I risk my life for someone I don't know?"

"Because your father is an anti-fascist, and because you lost your Diego in a stupid, useless war!"

Giustina fell silent and her eyes filled with tears.

"I'm sorry," said Attilio, placing a hand on her arm, "but you must help us or the Germans will kill us all."

"Who is this man you're bringing me?"

"He's the leader of a partisan group. The Germans and the Fascists are looking for him and they know he's in the area. In a fortnight's time he will escape to Bari on a motorised fishing boat. We have to help him, you have to help him. He's a brave man."

"But I've got no food for him. I can hardly feed myself… When will you bring him here?"

Attilio took her by the shoulders and hugged her.

"Thank you so much. He's right here, waiting."

"Outside? But where will he sleep? What can I give him to eat?"

"Oh, don't worry. He's frozen stiff and exhausted. He can sleep on the floor. I'll bring you some blankets tomorrow."

He went to the door, opened it and disappeared into the dark of the garden. "Giulio! Giulio!"

The outline of a man appeared in the doorway. Attilio pulled him in.

"This is Giulio, Giustina, please look after him. I'll be back tomorrow evening with blankets and something to eat. Thanks."

Before she could say anything, he had disappeared into the night. She and the man stood looking at each other.

He was tall, with a serious, strong-featured face and sweet chestnut eyes. It was difficult to guess his age, what with his straggly beard and unkempt dark hair. Giustina reckoned him to be somewhere in his thirties.

He looked at her, her shapely legs covered in black wool, her heavy socks on her little feet, that mass of jackets and coats from which emerged a pretty little face with big blue eyes, framed with brown curls.

"So you're Giulio." Giustina wanted to put an end to the embarrassing examination. "Have you had anything to eat?"

"It's not a problem, I can manage without."

"No, I'll make you something. I've not got a lot, but I can't send you to bed on an empty stomach."

While Giustina worked at the stove, Giulio moved round the room, taking note of everything. He gazed at the glass cupboard where Giustina had wedged some photographs between the wood frame and the glass. A smiling couple on their wedding day, a little baby boy with bright eyes, a man in uniform.

When Giustina turned to bring the food, she had prepared, to the table, she saw him engrossed in the photographs. She had the fleeting sensation of violation, that someone was invading her private life. She placed the boiled potatoes and frittata on a plate, and nearby a hunk of bread and a glass of red wine. Giulio sat down in silence. She remained standing.

"Won't you sit with me?"

She sat without speaking and looked at her guest. He ate in silence, in an elegant way. His white hands, with long, nervous fingers, were not those of a workman. Giustina considered her own hands, unobserved by her guest. They were small and strong, calloused with broken and dirty nails.

"This man is so different from me. What is he doing here, in my house?" she asked herself.

He seemed to guess what she was thinking. "I can never thank you enough for everything you're doing for me and the risk that you're running. What made you do it?"

"I'm not sure. Maybe it was Attilio. I trust him. Or maybe I just want to stand up to this German invasion that I don't like. First we're friends, now we're treated like enemies. They round up all the able-bodied men every week and make them work for them. There are only old men and women in the village."

When Giulio had finished eating, Giustina asked him to help her clear the little room, to move the bicycle and the sewing machine so she could prepare a makeshift bed for him. He helped her, constantly apologising for the trouble he was causing her. He said he would willingly sleep on the floor and that just to be indoors was a boon, given the freezing night outside. They brought clean sheets and a cushion into the room and Giustina went to fetch the blankets.

"Luckily, my mother gave me several blankets as a wedding gift. I bet she never thought they'd be warming a stranger!" she thought to herself while making the bed.

"Now go to sleep, Giulio. In the morning I'll be off early to the fields. I'll leave you something to eat for breakfast and lunch. I'll be back at sundown. Don't go out and don't let yourself be seen. There's almost no one round here, but it's silly to take risks. Goodnight."

She went into her room and hesitated for a moment in front of the door. Should she lock it? She braced herself and decided not to. Giulio had been brought here by Attilio; he was well mannered and kind; and then… she had seen how he looked at her, wrapped in her rags… Perhaps he lived in a big city with a beautiful, elegant wife who was waiting for him.

She got up at dawn. The door of the little room was ajar and she could hear the rhythmic breathing of the sleeping man. She left bread and fruit on the table, along with a slice of cheese and the flask of red wine that had been opened the night before. She left without making a sound.

She worked all day in the fields without so much as thinking about her guest. The winter fruits needed picking, and she had to fill dozens and dozens of baskets. At the end of the day, her boss gave her a basket with a little fruit, a few eggs and the luxury of a cauliflower.

She set off happily on her bicycle: she would have something to give her mysterious guest for dinner. When she opened her front door she could smell soup cooking. Surprised, she looked in to see Giulio in front of the stove, the fire lit and a pot boiling merrily. The table was set and wine already poured into the glasses.

Giulio looked amused as she approached.

"What have you done? Have you managed to cook something?"

"Attilio came by with some bread and vegetables. We can have a real feast tonight because I haven't eaten that cheese you left me. I want to share it with you."

They sat at the table and Giulio filled their bowls.

"I wanted to make myself useful. And at least you can have a hot meal after being out in the cold all day."

From the way he spoke and acted towards her, Giustina had the feeling that he knew a lot about her life, not just her heavy work in the fields, but also her loss of Diego, that tragedy that had marked her life.

They sat talking a while before bedtime. Giulio took a cigarette from his pocket but before lighting it asked, "Can I smoke? Or does it annoy you?"

She shook her head. Perhaps he was thinking of Diego and his tuberculosis.

"As much as you like. I like the smell of tobacco."

He looked into her eyes, perhaps trying to glimpse, in her expression, her longing for a memory.

After the mistrust of the first few days, Giustina had become used to the quiet, calm presence in her home. At sunset it was nice to go home to him after so many months of solitude, knowing that he, with Attilio's help, would have dinner ready for her. One evening there was even half a roast chicken on the table! She had got used to him, trusted him, put up with his eyes on her, sometimes insistently, on her waist that – despite the layers of clothing – seemed incredibly delicate from her agile movement. Often his eyes would fall on her woollen stockings. They were hardly elegant but they kept her warm. In the evenings he would try to find Radio London, giving news of the war.

She was also used to getting her news from various sources. Perhaps, she told herself, if she had listened to Radio London while Diego was alive, she could have had the truth about the war in Africa earlier, and participated in some way in his suffering.

The radio croaked out strange phrases: "The door is open", "The train is arriving", "The starlings have flown".

"What does it mean?" asked Giustina.

"They are coded messages that are broadcast to the Resistance in occupied territories. They might mean many things: the arrival of munitions, a warning of an air raid, partisans landing in the ports down south or freed Allied prisoners."

One evening, the weather was slightly warmer and they risked going out into the dark garden. They sat on the stoop, close together against the dampness of the evening, looking up at the stars. The cold light of the Moon lit the fields.

Giulio began to speak: "It seems impossible that so much time will have to pass before I return happily to a town, watch the shooting stars and take the hand of the girl I love. It makes me think of a poem by Paul Verlaine, 'Moonlight'."

Softly, as if speaking only to himself, he continued, "I don't remember the whole thing, just the last two verses:

'All sing in a minor key
Of victorious love and the opportune life,
They do not seem to believe in their happiness
And their song mingles with the moonlight,

"With the still moonlight, sad and beautiful,
That sets the birds dreaming in the trees
And the fountains sobbing in ecstasy,
The tall slender fountains among marble statues.'

Giustina listened in silence, watching his moonlit face. He

turned to look at her while he recited and tapped her on the hand when he had finished, as if looking for her approval.

"Who are you, Giulio? How old are you? Are you married? What did you do before the war?"

He wasn't expecting so many questions at that moment. He felt that she wanted to interrupt the romantic mood that the night had created between them.

"I'm a good person, or at least I think I am. I'm thirty-five, I'm not married, and since the war broke out I've not had a girl of my own. I was a teacher before the war and I hope I can go back to work when this is all over. I liked my job very much. Will that do? Have I answered all your questions?"

Giustina let out a laugh.

"You've answered them all. Did you teach little kids or the older ones?"

"The older ones. Now tell me about yourself. I know that you're only twenty-four, even if you try to act ten years older. I know that you're on your own and that you have a little boy, a very handsome one from his photograph, and that your mother looks after him. What else can you tell me?"

"I can tell you that in my heart and soul I'm at least thirty-four because the life I have led has been hard. I can't wait for the war to be over so I can find another job that will reunite me with Gabriele."

He took her hand and pulled it to his cheek. She let him because she understood that this was gesture of solidarity in her suffering. She had asked herself during the first few days how a young man could live in such close proximity to a young woman and yet behave so well, be so friendly. He was so different from the men and boys she had known, and so very different from Diego! She knew how Diego would have been in his place, how agitated and impatient. He would have wasted little time in trying to advance the relationship. For someone like Diego, action was the most important thing. Instead, Giulio liked to talk, mostly about politics but also about life, and she tried to follow him as best she could. He tried to explain why Italy had entered the war, and what the country hoped to gain from it. He told her about the aims of the Resistance in German-occupied Italy.

"The Allies are stuck between Termoli and Cassino and they will be stuck there for who knows how long. With winter approaching, it's difficult to see how an attack would be possible. But in a week I'll be gone and you can breathe easier. We're waiting for the new moon and I can make off on a fishing boat in the darkness. There will be a few British prisoners with me, and we'll try to get to Bari."

Giustina felt a strange sensation. Instead of being glad of her awkward guest's coming departure, she felt a deep pain inside her. She was used to Giulio, to his silences, to his sweet gazes and to his serious way of speaking. He seemed like a teacher all right, and one that she could learn a lot from!

She felt a sudden pang.

"If something happens to you," she said, "will I ever know? How will I know if you make it to Bari?"

"Do you really want to know? Is our struggle that important to you?"

"It is, Giulio, because for better or worse, I'm involved too now."

"Then I'll send you a message on Radio London. You'll hear the phrase 'Giulia has climbed the mountain' if I get to Bari. Are you happier now?"

"Yes," she admitted.

There were still two days until his departure. Attilio had come round late in the evening to tell her that two British servicemen who had escaped from a POW camp would be coming to the house and that they would leave with Giulio. She did not argue, knowing full well that she was already deep into this collaboration with the partisans.

The next night Attilio returned with the ex-prisoners around 11 o'clock. It was dark and no one had seen them. Giustina took them in and gave them a frugal supper. Giulio interpreted for them, speaking in English. Then they waited for night to fall. At one in the morning, Attilio, Giulio and the escaped prisoners prepared to go down to the beach where a boat was waiting for them. They would row away from the beach in silence and only when they were out to sea would they start the motor. The next step would be to rendezvous with a large fishing vessel that was waiting out in open water. They wrapped themselves up warmly in huge coats and put woollen caps on: it would be cold out at sea.

Giulio looked at Giustina inscrutably. He took her hand and held it between his for a time.

"I'll always be grateful," he said, "for everything you've done for me in these past few days. Perhaps you'll hear from me again. Goodbye for now. I hope you get the message that I've arrived safe in Bari."

He had whispered that last sentence.

Suddenly, he pulled her close to him, and Giustina felt his hands in her hair. Then he went out into the night with the others. He had his kitbag over his shoulder; Giustina knew it contained a pistol and a few items of clothing that he washed everyday and hung out to dry in the evening.

As he closed the door, she felt a knot in her throat. She ran to her room, threw herself on the bed and began to cry desperately. Her sobs shook her, and her tears soaked the pillow. Were these tears for Giulio? She was sure they weren't, they might have been for Diego, who died and left her alone with Gabriele; they were certainly for herself. Her loneliness weighed on her. Sometimes she would wake in the night, hoping that

Diego would be there to hold her and make her feel again the marvellous sensations of love.

A few days passed. Giustina listened to Radio London every evening. She had met Attilio in the village. He wasn't living in his house anymore, so scared was he of the round-ups the Germans were conducting. They met in the garage, where he was helping out his old boss.

"Will they have arrived yet? Do you know anything?"

"I don't, except that the fishermen on the boat said they had got as far as the big ship that was waiting for them. Apart from that, nothing. Are you worried?"

"I must admit that I am. A little."

"You like Giulio?"

Attilio was looking right at her. The question took her by surprise. She blushed deeply.

"What's got into you? Giulio is the leader of a band of partisans, and I, as a woman, no longer really exist. And you know it. And who is Giulio anyway? Do you know anything about him? He told me he taught older schoolchildren. Is he a high school teacher?"

"No, Giustina. Giulio Malinverni teaches physics at Pisa, one of the most important universities in all of Italy. He was an officer in the parachute regiment until the 8th of September, then he became a partisan and joined the Resistance in Central Italy. As far as I know, he's not married, but his family is one of the most important in Florence. He told me that he'll be dropped into the north of Italy to join up with the Resistance there. He's a very brave man and he believes in what he is doing. How did he behave towards you?"

"What is it you want to know, Attilio?"

"I don't know… Did he make any advances towards you, did he try to…?"

"Do you think I'm the sort of woman he'd do that with?" She looked sadly at her coat and her worn down shoes that she wore in the fields. "He was a gentleman, respectful and kind."

A week had passed since Giulio's departure and, in the evening, Giustina was sitting, ears glued to Radio London. There were lots of messages that evening, and almost at the end, between the static that interrupted the transmission she heard the phrase 'Giulia has climbed the mountain.' She felt her heart leap. That message was for her, and her alone. It was not a military communiqué, but a thought directed at her, to ease her anxiety. There was someone in the world, outside of her family, who cared about her. She mattered, ignorant, awkward and ugly as she was. She said nothing to Attilio when next they met at the garage. She thought that he might take that message the wrong way. Although he had never said anything to her, out of respect for Diego and his own sadness at his death, she understood that he had feelings for her, and that, with time, he could perhaps be more that friends with her.

Whenever Antonio, the boss, found an excuse to paw at Giustina's arm, Attilio took umbrage and tried to take him away from her. Hardly any time had passed since Diego had died and no one but no one was to upset her with their advances.

Now that Giulio was safe, Giustina thought about him often. She would have liked to be less ignorant, maybe to read and understand a few books, perhaps to learn about that beautiful poetry he had recited. She often encountered Attilio at the garage, and sometimes he would pop round to her house in the evenings. They would drink a glass of wine and keep each other company.

"I have to ask you a huge favour, Giustina," he said one afternoon, hesitation in his voice. "We have a store of weapons

– guns, bullets, grenades, that sort of thing – here in the village. We have to get them to a partisan command near where you work. Would you be willing to take them over there, a few at a time?"

"You're crazy. First you bring me a man all the Germans are searching for, then you ask me to carry weapons. Soon you'll be getting me to shoot Germans. You do know that I meet German patrols all the time where I work? If they found out I was ferrying weapons they'd kill me on the spot!"

"If it was that dangerous I wouldn't have asked you. They take less notice of a girl, and you only need carry a little at a time."

"It's too dangerous, Attilio. I need to think of Gabriele."

"If Giulio were here, would you say no to him?"

"What's Giulio got to do with it?"

"He's a partisan leader. He's hidden a whole arsenal of weapons."

Giustina fell silent and seemed to be thinking something over. "But why are you doing this?" she asked. "Why are you taking such risks?"

"I'm in a partisan band that is in revolt against the German occupation. There are officers, soldiers and police in our group."

"But what can you do? You can't take them on with guns, they'd destroy you."

"We're not that crazy. We only shoot when we have to. The weapons might be useful for those who have to retreat up into the mountains, up the Gran Sasso or around Ascoli Piceno. But what we're doing can help the Allies: we keep watch on the German movements night and day, on their columns moving to the front line or up north. In some places we even clear mines. The bands in Central Italy are in contact with one another and those closest to the city can try to sabotage roads, railways and communications."

Giustina had listened to all this without comment. "Okay. What do I have to do?"

"I'll bring you stuff every evening, mostly bullets and grenades. You have to put them in a shack on the road to Sant'Omero, about a mile from the fork that takes you to your work. That's why we thought of you. Do you think you can do it?"

"I can try, Attilio. But if I meet a German or a Fascist patrol, I don't think I'll be able to stay calm. I'm pretty frightened already."

He took her hand and squeezed it with affection.

"You are a brave woman, and you've been through a lot. I'm sure you can do it. I'll bring you the first batch tonight and tell you how to handle it."

She spent the rest of the afternoon in a state of tension, unable to tidy the house even. The road to Sant'Omero was often used by the Germans. The fact that she frequently walked there just after dawn, when there was no one else around scared her even more. That evening, Attilio brought her the first consignment, two boxes of bullets and four grenades.

"Handle these carefully, don't touch the pin at the top or it'll go off. Please, Giustina, don't have me worried for you."

The next day, at dawn, Giustina got her bicycle ready. She placed the box and the grenades in the basket that sat on top of the front mudguard. She covered them with a scarf, placing bread and fruit – a little too much for her lunch – and a full bottle of wine on top of that. She set off, trying to pedal, her legs trembling.

There was no one on the road. She pedalled fast, past the fork that took her to the farm. She rode on for a mile before she came to the farm that Attilio had told her about. The farmhouse itself seemed to be deep asleep. She knocked softly at the door.

"Who is it?"

"I've been sent by Attilio Di Mizio. I have something to deliver."

A man opened the door and ushered her in, bicycle and all.

They were in a large, sparsely furnished kitchen. The man took the items carefully from the basket and deposited them in an opening in a wall, hidden by a cupboard. He thanked her with a smile, saying, "I'll see you tomorrow."

Giustina set off quickly. She was calmer now and would be able to deal with any 'nasty encounters' that came her way. She got to the field and began her day's work. She felt a strange sensation; it was like when, as a child, she had been up to something and was now waiting for her mother to find out.

Every evening she would wait for Attilio with trepidation. He would always arrive punctually and present her with another consignment of ammunition. Carrying weapons had become almost second nature for her. She would often pass German patrols. She would pass them with a smile and a wave.

Early one morning, however, a patrol stopped her. There had been a shooting the night before and the man had died. She didn't know his name, and her first thought had been of Giulio: "I hope it wasn't him!" She had calmed herself down, knowing that Giulio must either still be in Bari or already have parachuted into the north of the country.

A German soldier walked over to the bicycle and put his hand on the handlebars. "What is this?" he asked, gesturing at the basket.

Giustina's heart beat so fast she felt it would burst from her chest. She tried to pull herself together. She smiled mischievously. "It's a bomb. Can't you see it's my lunch? I'm a farm hand and I'm expected in the fields. Can I go? The boss will fine me if I'm late."

The German, who understood Italian, waved her on. She headed off slowly, without showing any great hurry. She could feel the eyes of the patrol on her. While pedalling, she turned and waved them goodbye.

When she was out of sight, she stopped for a moment to collect herself together. Her heart was still beating wildly. These deliveries continued for a long time. Giustina often met with patrols, but the Germans would greet her warmly now that they knew her. She felt a pang of pity and tenderness for those young men. Like Diego, they were victims of circumstances greater than themselves. In all likelihood, one of them, like Diego, would not return home. She felt a great hatred rise up in her heart, a great and furious hatred against the war, against this absurd disaster that tore through the civilised world, forcing men – perhaps fundamentally good men – to commit vile, absurd, violent acts against each other.

She often met Attilio in the evening, at Antonio's garage, on her way back from the fields. She would stop to chat with both of them. One evening, when they were alone for a moment, Attilio pulled her aside. "Hey, Giustina, how would you like to see a boatload of munitions blow up?"

"What do you mean?"

Before answering, Attilio looked about him. "Tomorrow afternoon the Americans are going to try to bomb a raft that is loaded with ammunition and explosives at San Benedetto del Tronto. I'd like to see it, but I can't let myself be seen in broad daylight. Do you want to go?"

"Where do I have to go?"

"You know the bluff at Colonnella that they call the Semaphore? You can enjoy the show from there. Can you get there?"

She stood in thought for a moment.

"If it's early in the afternoon, I'll have to ask the boss to let me away early. But how did you find out about it?"

Attilio came closer and whispered: "It was us. We tipped the Americans off."

Giustina said her goodbyes and headed home. She thought about how the bombing would harm innocent people, and her disgust for the war deepened all the more. All the same, she asked to be released early the next day and, after a hurried lunch, she left the fields. She pedalled hard, dismounting when she reached the path up to the Semaphore. She knew the place well because Diego, looking for a place to flirt with her, had taken her there often in Antonio's sidecar. She reached the top of the headland and passed the concrete building that had perhaps once been a lighthouse. Looking out to sea, she could make out the port of San Benedetto del Tronto quite clearly.

Back in the house, she had dug out Diego's old binoculars. She now held them up to her eyes and focused them on the harbour. There were a couple of fishing boats and small cargo steamers bobbing there. On the right was a large raft, covered with a military tarpaulin. She lay back on the tall grass and waited.

Around half past three, she heard the unmistakable sound of the American bombers, probably laden with bombs. She had learned by now to tell the difference between planes that were fully loaded and those which had already dropped their death-dealing cargo. She remained prone so that she would not be spotted and looked through the binoculars. Soon the American planes could be seen with the naked eye.

The first shots were fired by the German anti-aircraft guns. The bombers dived and two of them dropped their bombs. The first landed in the sea, causing a great column of water to rise up, but the second hit the centre of the raft, which then leapt in the air. The explosion came a moment later. It deafened Giustina, who covered her ears automatically. The powerful blast reverberated around the mute hills. The American planes regained altitude as the German anti-aircraft barrage grew still more intense.

A sudden cry escaped Giustina. One of the planes had been hit and, with the tail on fire, was falling towards the sea. She brought her hands to her mouth and began to pray.

"Dear God! There is a pilot in that plane, I don't know whether alive or dead. Please do something for him!"

Something broke off from the plane that became a man dangling from a parachute, floating slowly down towards the sea. The wind pushed him in the direction of the beach where a number of German soldiers awaited. Through the binoculars, Giustina watched anxiously as he hit the waves and freed himself from the parachute and began to swim towards the safety of the beach. The Germans waited and, when he got close to them, a burst of machine-gun fire finished him off. Giustina wanted to cry out, to shout that he was a prisoner of war, that he had surrendered and was swimming towards them.

She felt an immense sadness that took her breath away, struck her from her mouth to her stomach. She thought of a mother or a wife or a girlfriend, far away in America, receiving the sterile telegram of notification, the last news she would have of her boy: killed while carrying out his duty in the service of his country. Later, when Attilio came round to see her in the evening, he found her in floods of tears. It took her some time to explain to him, in mangled sentences, what she had seen.

"War is a terrible thing," said Attilio, trying to console her, "and the Germans are becoming more cruel and vicious because they understand they are losing the war. Can I have a glass of wine?"

She looked at him, surprised. "Do you need a drink? Has it got to you, too?"

"Well, I'm shaken up, certainly, but it's something else that's worrying me. The night after next, I'm to join up with a group of patriots to block off one of the roads through the hills and prevent a German supply convoy reaching the front at Vasto."

Giustina's eyes widened.

"How will you do that?"

"First we block the road with tree trunks, then we blow up the bridge over the stream. They'll have to go down the coast then, and there will be bombers waiting for them to the south."

"How many of you will there be?"

"Seven altogether. Some to close off the road with the tree trunks and others to blow up the bridge."

"It'll be a massacre. They'll cut you up with their guns," said Giustina, her voice trembling.

"I don't think so," replied Attilio. "Those in charge of the tree trunks are to do their bit as soon as night falls and then go and hide. Then this bomb expert – you don't know him – and I will blow up the bridge while the Germans are wondering who's blocked the road. Then we escape into the dark countryside. There'll be no moon and we'll know better than the Germans how to move about in that country."

Giustina kept quiet while he spoke. The silence lasted a long time. Then she spoke. "Could I come with you?"

Attilio looked at her in surprise.

"No, Giustina, this isn't the time. It's a dangerous situation, and a girl might get panicked…"

Giustina interrupted him.

"If the girl doesn't get panicked when a German asks her what's in the basket that she has filled with grenades, she must be a pretty special girl." She looked at him with a pride that had grown from her speech.

Attilio replied, hesitantly. "But are you sure you want to? After we blow the bridge, the Germans will be after us. We'll have to hide from them in the fields. Do you really want to come with us?"

"Certainly." Giustina's tone was firm.

So they made arrangements for the night mission. Attilio would wait for her at ten before going on to the bridge. That night Giustina could not sleep and the next day she was quiet and anxious at work. Now that the moment was arriving, she wondered if she had done the right thing, going off with Attilio to be a guerrilla. She might be alone just now, but she had a child who depended on her. What had urged her to do it? She looked for an answer and, in her insecurity, she convinced herself that it was a response to the killing of the young American pilot. It had been a moment that kindled a great deal of anger and the desire to react against this cruel occupation in her heart. She had to do something.

The night of the mission came round fast. It was a crisp winter's night, dark and moonless. Giustina wore a thick woollen coat, a beret that she had crocheted herself and a stout pair of shoes. She met Attilio at the appointed place and the two of them set off along paths they knew through the fields towards the bridge over the stream. The road that ran alongside the hills was not completely asphalted, and the trees and bushes protected the military vehicles from observation. They stopped near the bridge. A group of five or six men were already at work moving the tree trunks into place and tying them together. The silence of the night was total, and the men worked quietly and carefully. They walked on to the bridge, where a man was placing sticks of dynamite at the base of the piers and on the arch.

"What can we do?" asked Attilio.

"Get the fuse ready. And don't put it on the ground, it'll get wet with all this rain we've had.

Attilio and Giustina made a small path of dry stones over which the fuse could run, hidden in the bushes. Giustina's actions were firm and decisive, but inside her heart was beating fast and her voice trembled slightly when she asked, "What way do we run when we light the fuse?"

"You run as fast as you can back to your house! Remember to crouch while you run because the Germans might start shooting at head height as soon as they see the tree trunks on the road. And don't look back. Not even if you hear shooting. Not even if you hear someone… getting shot."

She looked up at Attilio in surprise but he didn't notice; the night was dark. Once the preparations were made they crouched in the bushes. The men who had laid the roadblock vanished into the night.

After maybe half an hour, they could hear the first sounds of the approaching vehicles. The Germans were coming.

The sound got closer and the head of the column appeared suddenly around the corner, dimly lit by the dipped headlights of the motorbikes, officers' cars and trucks. There was a screeching of brakes and the column stopped at the roadblock. Excited voices, orders cracked like whips in the night. Some officers got out of their cars and walked to the front of the convoy to inspect the tree trunks.

"Now!" hissed Attilio to the man who had placed the dynamite on the bridge. "Light the fuse!"

At the touch of the match, the fuse took light. The flame snaked quickly towards the bridge.

"Go!" he urged.

The three of them ran for the countryside in different directions. At that moment, a tremendous blast shook the air for hundreds of yards around. Giustina looked over her shoulder to see the bridge exploding into thousands of pieces. She seemed to be flying across the ground.

Then a searchlight lit up the whole area and a machinegun fired.

Giustina, who was running with her head down, felt suddenly exposed by the sound of the shooting. She instinctively fled to a field planted with vines where she could hide from the German soldiers, advancing quickly across the countryside. More shots, and then a stifled scream. Giustina put her hand to her mouth to stop herself from crying out: she was sure one of her comrades had been hit. She kept running with the speed of a cat. She heard the barked orders of the pursuing Germans.

By now she was panting. She had run a quarter of a mile and suddenly her legs failed her. She tripped and fell without a sound into a ditch, muddy and wet from the rain. She was sure she was lost; her last thought was to cover herself with a leafy branch to hide from the hunters. Muddy and wet, she covered her head with her arm and shivered in the ditch, awaiting her fate.

Soon, she heard the footsteps of a German soldier. She was amazed that he couldn't hear her heartbeat. He passed by. She stayed in that position for what seemed forever. As the sky brightened before dawn, she heard the noise of the German convoy backing up and turning round.

She still didn't move for half an hour. Then she lifted her head slowly to check if there was anyone around. There wasn't. She hurried home, caked in mud. She arrived at dawn and, resisting the temptation to collapse into bed, looked a moment in the mirror. She acted decisively, taking off her muddy clothes and throwing them into the spring in the garden and thus removing all trace of her nocturnal adventure. Looking at last night's outfit in the water, it struck her that its presence there practically amounted to a confession. She ran to the house and threw in three jumpers, two dresses and another wool coat. She added another couple of items of underwear. She cleaned her shoes carefully and then, since the day had almost begun, got ready for work at the farm. On the way, she noticed more soldiers than usual at the checkpoints. She stuck a smile on her face and passed by unmolested.

But in the fields, the women were full of excitement. They whispered that partisans had blown up a bridge, that one of them had been shot dead by the Germans. Giustina was sick to her soul, worried that the dead man was Attilio. She steeled herself against revealing her state of mind. She worked the whole day in silence and decided not to visit Antonio's garage that night, in case the Germans had worked out Attilio's connection with him, if indeed it was Attilio they had shot.

So she got home exhausted, pedalling the last stretch with great weariness. She stopped when she saw the two men in front of her house. One was a German soldier, the other a member of the Fascist militia whom she knew by sight. She approached and said politely, "Are you waiting for me? Can I help you?"

The militiaman replied, "Won't you invite us in, Mrs Moretti? We need to speak to you."

She opened the door and had the two men sit down. They looked around suspiciously.

The militiaman asked, "Is there anyone here living with you?"

"With me?" asked Giustina, astonished, "Are you not aware, comrade, that I am a war widow? And that because I have to work in the fields, I've left my son Gabriele with his grandparents? I see him in Tortoreto on Saturdays and Sundays."

"Can we have a look around the house?"

"Feel free! It's a pretty small house…"

They peered into the bedroom and the spare room but found nothing in particular. They stopped in front of the door to the garden.

"Where does this door lead? It's locked, can we have it opened?"

"Of course. It leads to my garden."

She opened the door and the men looked around outside. A high wire fence protected her little patch of land from the surrounding country.

"No one could get over that…" one of them commented.

"Why would you climb it when you could use the door?" asked Giustina sardonically.

"You've got quite a lot of washing here, Mrs Moretti!"

"Absolutely. I managed to get it done yesterday. This week all we've had is rain, so I used the good weather while it was here." She was thinking what a good idea it had been to wash all those clothes. Who knows what they would have said if there had been just her dress, her coat and a pair of woollen socks! The men left soon afterwards, leaving her puzzled. Why had they come to search her house? What had they suspected? She had not had the courage to ask them herself why they had come. Perhaps they thought someone was hidden in the house or in the garden because her house was so far from the road? She would have to be more careful in future so as not to compromise Attilio, if he was still alive.

In the end, she didn't go to the garage, but went to the piazza by the station with the excuse of getting something to eat. There she could listen to the gossip of the women and old men of the town.

"Is it true they shot a partisan?"

"Yes, some stranger. They're going nuts trying to find out who he was but they've got nowhere. It must be someone from outside."

Giustina breathed a sigh of relief. Attilio was safe and probably hiding.

The dead man must be the young engineer who had set the charges on the bridge. She had only met him that night, but his death made a deep impression on her.

Late on the following morning, the boss brought news to the women in the fields. The German column that was forced to go down the coast had been attacked and destroyed by American planes before it reached Termoli.

"What happened? Were any of our men wounded?" Giustina asked shakily.

"Three truckloads of ammunition were blown up, two Germans were killed and several injured. Although they were machine-gunned, many of them were able to hide in the trees. No Italians were wounded. The road after Silvi Marina has been closed off for now."

Giustina kept quiet.

Giustina didn't see Attilio for a couple of weeks. At first she wasn't concerned, but then the long silence began to worry her and she became anxious that the Germans had captured him and sent him to a work camp. So late one evening when he knocked on her door, she was unable to control herself and threw her arms around him. Attilio hugged her back and he choked a little as he spoke.

"I was so frightened when they started shooting. I've heard about Salvatore, and I'm very sorry. He had a wife and baby, just a couple of months old, back in Sicily…"

"Who will tell them that he's dead?" asked Giustina anxiously.

"Someone will tell the family, don't worry. How are you doing? Are you still frightened?"

"I'm not frightened, I'm angry. I'm so mad at these thugs coming into our country and killing us. It's not as if we've been in Germany terrorising them!"

"I heard that they came to search the house. Don't worry about that. They didn't think you'd hidden someone, just that someone might have hidden in your garden without your knowledge."

"That's a relief! That means we can organise another sortie against them!"

Attilio smiled at her enthusiasm. There would be plenty of opportunities for her.

The first one came when a dozen or so escaped Allied prisoners had to be embarked on a fishing boat. This was similar, in actual fact, to Giulio's escape that Giustina had been involved in. Because she drew the least suspicion, it was her job to plan the means and the night of the escape with the fishermen. Just as with Giulio, this operation was successful.

However, in December, the Germans – with the help of Italians loyal to the collapsed Fascist State – had begun to round up men to build coastal fortifications. In these round-ups, several men who were anti-fascist agents were arrested, along with Italian soldiers who had not enlisted with Mussolini's Republic of Salò. Many of these men were never heard of again. Some people said they had been taken to concentration camps in Germany or in Venezia Giulia.

The round-ups generally took place at dawn, when the raiders could count on the sleepiness of their quarry. The SS encircled the town where the operation was to take place, blocking the roads in and out. The result was that the whole population lived in anxiety, fear and in unconscious expectation of these events. The women would try to warn the men, who would try to escape, usually falling into the traps set by the German soldiers.

The men, once captured, were brought before the German authorities, were identified and then sent to work preparing defences on the coast and hills. A truck would pick them up before dawn and bring them back at sundown every day. Anyone trying to flee could only make for the mountains, because he would be shot if found.

That morning, Giustina woke to a strange noise. There were

whistles and quiet, barked orders breaking the silence of the darkness. Although her house was a hundred yards from the road, she could hear hurried steps; it seemed that someone was running through her garden. She got up, shivering, from the bed and listened.

Looking at the clock, she saw it was half-past four. In an hour she would have to get moving to go to work. She dressed quickly and, on the stroke of five, she headed for the Nazionale with her bicycle.

Abrupt orders stopped her. A German soldier told her to stay where she was. She tried to explain that she had to get to work on the country roads, but he made her turn back. She went back to the house but remained attentive. She heard voices, a truck going by, orders being shouted. "A round-up. The first one here in Giulianova. I hope Attilio didn't sleep in the village last night. What will the boss say when he sees I'm not at work? I'll probably lose a day's pay."

She tried to spend the morning tidying the house, and ventured out only in the afternoon. Everything seemed normal and quiet. The village seemed deserted. Hesitantly, she headed for Diego's house, where his mother and sister might be able to explain what had gone on.

She found Silvana in tears. Giustina's heart seemed to be bursting in her chest.

"What's happened? What are you crying for?" she asked her sister-in-law. Silvana put her arms round her.

"They rounded up all the men this morning, including my Alfredo. He was at home and although he's already forty, the Germans took him away. My own fiancé! He'll have to work for them as if he were a prisoner! If he tries to get away, they'll shoot him! And my boss, Sante Mariotti, they've taken him to Teramo. They caught him in the fields where he was trying to hide."

"What will happen to him?" breathed Giustina.

"Who knows? Maybe they'll take him up north or to Germany. But the worst thing is that someone painted a cross on each of the houses supposed to belong to partisans. Attilio's house was one of them. I hope they haven't caught him, although I did see him late last night in the village…"

Giustina had turned to stone. Attilio's arrest would mean an interruption of the partisan struggle and greater difficulties ahead. She returned Silvana's embrace.

"Don't cry. Alfredo is here, at least, even if he has to work for the Germans. I'm more worried about signor Mariotti…"

Giustina's work with the partisans was far from finished. For six months she helped prisoners escape from the beaches of Abruzzo: resistance fighters, escaped POWs, officers deserting the Fascists. She had plenty to do. One evening, Attilio came to see her late at night wearing a worried expression. She understood straight away.

"What have you got for me?"

Attilio sat down, drank the wine Giustina had brought for him and tried to explain what he had found himself involved with.

"Tomorrow evening we have to get someone away at all costs. He is a British officer, high up in Intelligence. The Germans captured him in Termoli four days ago and were taking him up north to interrogate him when our friends rescued him near Roseto yesterday evening. Now he's in hiding with a farmer and I'll bring him to you tomorrow for you to take him to the beach."

"But I'm working tomorrow! How am I to find a fisherman to take him?"

"I've already seen to that. Gaetano will be waiting with his brother at one in the morning."

She thought for a moment, then asked, "Is he important, this guy? What's his name?"

"Yes, he's a British colonel. He's indispensable to the resistance near the front. I'd rather not tell you his name. You will take him to the boat tomorrow."

Attilio got up, stroked Giustina's cheek and went away in silence.

She was left alone, sitting at the table, thinking. She wasn't afraid, even though she was always afflicted by a certain sense of anxiety when a dangerous operation came to a head. It was her practice now to use the last underpass under the railway when she went with her charges to the beach. It was lonely and dirty, and you rarely saw anyone there during the day because it was smelly and full of rubbish.

Since she had joined the resistance her life had certainly changed. It was an important part of her life that her family knew nothing about for the moment. She could tell her son about it one day, assuming that she got out of it alive. Sometimes she thought back on her life before, when she was newly married and she thought only of her house and her love for her husband. That happiness had been short-lived because Diego had been called up. What followed had been a slow, agonising tragedy.

The next evening at midnight, Attilio knocked quietly at the door. She opened up and, right behind Attilio, a strange man pushed his way into the house. The mysterious British colonel commanded her full attention. He was very tall and thin, his face was unfriendly, an impression accentuated by his thin lips and clear light-blue eyes. His hair was a reddish-blond and was worn with a side parting. His complexion was reddened by the cold. The civilian clothes he was wearing fitted him badly: the jacket was too big and the trousers too short. Attilio stayed only a few minutes, just long enough to remind her apprehensively,

"This is a very important man, Giustina. He must get away, at all costs. He has already eaten, so you don't have to worry about that."

Once Giustina had seen Attilio off, she turned to see the curious, cold eyes of the colonel on her. She blushed and, with a gesture, invited him to take a seat. He understood and sat at the table. Giustina filled a glass with wine and offered it to him, theatrically shivering to show him it would warn him up. He drank it and sighed, "Excellent!"

Giustina had studied English for a couple of years at school, but now she had the opportunity to use it, not a single word came to her. She plucked up courage none the less to speak to the colonel. "Mio nome è Giustina." He didn't move. He hadn't understood. She prepared herself carefully, trying to speak clearly and above all not to make a mistake: "My name is Giustina. And you?"

He smiled and answered, "George."

They went on looking at each other in silence for ten more minutes. Then she got up, put on a heavy coat and covered her head with her beret.

"It's time to go," she said in Italian, and he understood this time. "Good."

They went out into the dark moonless and starless night. The weather didn't promise much for the following day: the sky was covered with black clouds. Giustina led the way and the colonel followed. They came to the underpass, the furthest from the port, the one Giustina always used. She took his hand because there was rubbish strewing the ground.

Suddenly there was the light sound of a footstep in the culvert. Giustina reacted immediately. She came close to the colonel and whispered, "Put your arms round me."

She sensed rather than saw the astonished expression of the colonel. However, he understood almost immediately and pulled her to him, even putting his own head in her hair to hide his own height. "Excuse me..." he whispered.

They remained entwined for a few moments before the shadow of a man appeared in the light glow of the entrance to the tunnel. He clearly knew the terrain, because he had dismounted from his bicycle and was pushing it by hand. Giustina's heart was in her throat now, and she could feel the colonel's heart beating hard next to her. The man with the bicycle had turned his headlamp off, so he couldn't quite make out who the kissing couple were, although he slowed as he passed them before increasing his pace again.

Giustina and the colonel remained frozen for a few more moments and then detached themselves from each other's grip the better to hear the man's footsteps. Silence. Joining hands again, they walked on to the beach where their tardiness had worried the fishermen. The first of them pushed the boat out and the second signalled the colonel to get in. He turned to Giustina, took her hand and brought it to his lips. "Thank you. Goodnight."

She smiled and murmured, "Ciao Georgio. Good luck!"

She stood on the beach and watched the two rowers pull the boat silently out to sea.

A couple of days later, Giustina came home from work to find Silvana waiting for her at the gate. She was surprised and came and embraced her sister-in-law. It was not often that the two of them met, partly because of the blackouts, which meant it was advisable to be home before dark. Giustina ushered her in. She asked her all about the family and talked about Gabriele, who resembled Diego in lots of little ways. Silvana didn't seem to want to talk much and so Giustina pressed her, suspicious, "Why did you come? Did you want to tell me something? Is someone sick? How is your mother?"

Silvana became calmer.

"No, we're all fine, given how things are. I get to see Alfredo in the evenings. It's something else, and I don't know how to talk to you about it. Pietruccio came to see me yesterday evening. You know Pietruccio, the tailor who's working for the Germans now as well? Anyway, he told me that the other night, around one in the morning, he thought he saw you with a man he didn't recognise. You were kissing in the underpass, that filthy one where no one ever goes. He thought he recognised your hair even in the dark. Was it you? What were you doing with that man? And at that hour?"

Giustina had learned how to control her nerves in the last few months. She burst out laughing.

"Someone saw me snuggling with a man in the middle of the night? In that rubbish tip under the railway? That's a romantic spot for a couple of lovers! Oh Silvana, your brother has been dead less than a year, and I have no desire to find anyone new. And even if I were to feel that desire, would I not be better bringing someone here? No one ever comes round here."

Silvana breathed a sigh of relief and confessed, "I almost believed Pietruccio, even if it seemed impossible."

She hugged Giustina, who went on, "My heart is dead, Silvana, you must know that. And besides, what man would want me now? I'm in rags, worn out and an absolute mess."

"Yes, I suppose you're right, Giustina. Let me have a glass of wine and I'll be off. It's getting dark and I don't want the soldiers seeing me out and about."

With Silvana gone, Giustina had time to worry.

A couple of weeks went by without her hearing from Attilio. While she had plenty to occupy herself with her work and her chores around the house, her thoughts often strayed to the strange British colonel who had almost ended up exposing her. Attilio turned up one evening when she was already thinking of going to bed, tired after a day's work. He took the glass of wine she offered him and finally decided to give her the good news: the colonel had arrived safely in Termoli.

"What did you do to him?" he asked.

She arched her eyebrows questioningly. "Why?"

"Because he asked me to thank you with a kiss."

She smiled brightly. "That's our secret."

The conversation broke off as Attilio tried to work out what that mysterious phrase might mean. Giustina interrupted the suspense to tell him that someone had recognised her in the underpass that night, despite the darkness. Attilio looked frightened.

"Are you sure?"

"Yes, my sister-in-law came to tell me. The tailor who lives up near her said he saw me with a man. I denied everything, I even laughed, but I think that for a while we shouldn't use that route to get people to the boats. Remember... the tailor also dresses the Germans."

Attilio seemed upset, then genuinely sorry.

"This is terrible. I've put you in a horrible position and I'm sorry for that. We'll have to stop that activity for the time being, and possibly for good. But I have another job for you..."

"Through another underpass?" interrupted Giustina.

"No, my dear, it's something that you'll have to do during the day, perhaps next Sunday."

Giustina interrupted again. "You know that I see Gabriele on a Sunday. It's the only day I can."

"You'll have to make this sacrifice. You have to go to the old part of the cemetery in Mosciano and look for the grave of Carlo Plinio Maineri, born 1854, died 1918. It's the twelfth tombstone on your right as you go in. You have to wait there for a man.

He's about thirty, and he'll ask you if it's your grandfather you're visiting. You then have to give him this envelope. It's full of counterfeit documents that will allow him to get to the north to join up with partisans there. He's American, but speaks Italian. You can have a look at the documents if you like, but keep them well hidden until Sunday and be careful. There might be other people in the cemetery."

She took the envelope and looked at the documents inside. They were for a certain Antonio Porretti, born 1914 in Parma and resident in that city. Along with the document was a letter of introduction for the chief of police in Turin, which explained that he was a detective in charge of a special investigation. The letter bore the official stamp of the German command of the city. She re-closed the envelope and asked, "Are they both fakes?"

"Absolutely."

"And if the Germans do their checks?"

"They'll find nothing wrong. We have good friends in Turin as well."

Attilio left, warning Giustina to be extremely careful.

Sunday arrived almost too quickly. Giustina rode her bike up the road to Mosciano. As she pedalled she thought of Gabriele who would be expecting her arrival and who would be disappointed not to see her. She decided then that if this meeting with the American didn't take all morning, she would go to her son in the early afternoon. She had hidden the documents inside one of her stockings, against her thigh, held in place by two garters. She felt sure that the Germans would never look there.

She didn't know where the cemetery was in Mosciano, so she had to stop and ask a woman she met on the outskirts of the town. Her basket contained the only flowers she could find: there wasn't a lot of choice in February, so she had a nice big clump of mimosa from her garden and a few sprays of ivy leaves.

Following the woman's directions, she reached the cemetery. She went in and headed for the part that seemed to her to be the oldest. She found the correct row on the right and began to count. When she reached the twelfth tombstone, CARLO PLINIO MAINERI printed in capital letters as Attilio had told her, her heart skipped. She looked around, but there was no one near her.

There was nothing in the vase that sat in front of the stone, except for dust and a few cobwebs. Since she had brought flowers, she went and found a tap to wash and fill the old vase. She put the flowers in it, and placed it respectfully in front of the stone.

There was not a soul anywhere around her. Looking at her watch, she saw it was 10:30. She crossed herself and recited a prayer, seeing as she was there. She jumped when a young man's voice asked her, "Is this your grandfather's grave, miss?"

Giustina raised her eyes to look the man over carefully. She was not certain that this was the American she was waiting for: he was well dressed, almost elegant, wearing a Loden coat and a felt hat with the brim pulled slightly down. Seeing her uncertainty, the man smiled and said, "Attilio sent me. Are you Giustina?"

She relaxed. "I was a bit frightened, sorry. I wasn't sure that you were the right man... you look too... elegant."

The man laughed. "You've forgotten I'm a police detective on a secret mission!"

He turned to the gravestone and said, "This isn't your grandfather. He was mine, even if he died when I was four. I remember him visiting us in Chicago. He was a good granddad, and I was his first grandson. I was named after him."

"Your name is Carlo Plinio?" Giustina asked in amazement.

"No," he laughed, "My name is Charlie Edward, but everyone calls me Eddie."

A woman had appeared at the end of the row and the two fell silent. Eddie made the sign of the cross and joined his hands in prayer. Giustina copied him. As the woman passed them, she slowed down to read the inscription that the two young people were praying before. She was quite surprised to see the date on the tombstone. All the same, she kept on walking and made her way down another row.

"How did you get here?" Giustina asked.

"How did you make it here?" Eddie asked in response.

"I have my bicycle," she said, pointing to it.

"A friend gave me a lift. He's waiting for me outside on a cart pulled by the most beautiful horse. Back at his house, my motorbike is waiting. I don't fancy riding all the way to Bologna on horseback! Right, you can give me the documents now."

Giustina lifted her skirt rather self-consciously. She loosened the top garter that held the documents in place and took out the envelope. Despite having tried her best to cover herself with her coat, she could not prevent Eddie from seeing a flash of her pink-fleshed thigh. He took the envelope and said, with a mischievous expression, "I'll take special care of these, now I've seen where they were hidden."

Giustina reddened. "Are all Americans so gauche, or are you the exception?"

"We're not all gauche, but when we are handed something that has been kept so secret and so … warm, it's hard to react otherwise. Please pardon me, Giustina, but you are a beautiful lady."

"How do you know my name?"

"Attilio told me."

"And did he also tell you that my husband died in the war, two years ago?"

There was bitterness in Giustina's voice and Eddie felt suddenly guilty. He took her hand and brought it to his lips. "I didn't know that and I'm sorry," he said, saddened. "War is an ugly thing and I myself don't know if I'm going to get home alive. This mission is a risky one. I just wanted to compliment you, Giustina. You really are beautiful."

She held out her hand to him to let him know he was forgiven. They left the cemetery together, Giustina pushing her bicycle alongside her. They said goodbye at the exit. Before heading off, she watched Eddie jump onto the trap, surprised that it had not been requisitioned by the Germans.

As she pedalled along the Adriatica towards Tortoreto, she thought of how the war had brought her into contact with people from such different places, so far away from what was her world before the fighting started.

The end of the harsh winter saw the Allies recommence their offensive; things were moving on the Italian front. There was great expectation among the people: the German occupation had been difficult to take and, at times, tragic. The winter had seen never-ending round-ups, men taken away from the villages and forced to work on building fortifications on the coast or air defences for San Benedetto del Tronto and Giulianova. The only ones who escaped the net were those who hid by day in niches in the walls or in attics and came out only at night. Attilio was one of these, and he often came to see Giustina over the fields. He still helped Antonio, who built him a proper little hiding hole in the back of the garage.

Liberation finally came in June of 1944. The first troops to arrive in the village were Italian paratroopers attached to the British 5th Corps and members of the 2nd Corps of the Polish Army.

In Giulianova there were celebrations in the main square and everyone was delighted to see the streets full of young men again after so long. Among those present were all the partisans who had operated in the area. Giustina was there, Attilio having rushed to fetch her in Antonio's sidecar, pinning a rosette in the colours of the Italian flag on her chest. She was shy of the attention and avoided her friends' questions about her difficult missions and her gun-running.

The front had passed on, but the war was not yet over. The first days of June saw the Allies landing in Normandy and heading for Paris. Sometimes Giustina's thoughts reached out to Giulio. He was still in the north of Italy where, according to Attilio, the struggle was becoming crueller as the Germans recognised their coming defeat.

April 1945 saw the end of the war for the Italians, at least. It had been a total war, affecting people all over the world and with an enormous cost to humanity. Millions of lives had been lost. But more than that, old political balances, customs, habits and dearly-held beliefs had been shattered.

Even the little villages of Abruzzo had been changed forever, with soldiers of so many different nationalities passing through. The villagers, having had to deal with the hostile and overbearing Germans, now found themselves in the company of Americans, British, Polish and French, all with their own ideas, habits and ways of behaving that were strange to them. They even saw, to their great surprise, women auxiliaries and officers!

The end of the war had allowed some foods to come back into the lives of Italians, in particular coffee and butter. And chocolate, whose very taste many people had forgotten. But American films arrived as well, and these offered the people – used to a simple life that was much the same as those of the people around them – a glimpse of the extraordinary. They showed examples of freedom of expression, freedom of conduct and, most importantly, a completely different view of how a woman should live her life. Giustina, like many others, felt she was breathing a new air and compared herself, often frivolously, with these feminine, free, independent and happier prototypes. She began to realise her own limitations, the difficulty she had in accepting ideas from a world that was so different from the one she had been living in, in understanding points of view, even simple ones, which were grounded in a culture deeper than her own.

She had left the *liceo tecnico* in the third year and had not studied since, even though her parents were ready to make any sacrifice necessary for her to extend her cultural horizons as far as she wished. But she was a simple girl back then, and marriage for her – as for many others – was the most she wanted for herself. Since closing her schoolbooks, she told herself sadly, she had read practically nothing. The only exceptions were the newspapers she would read now and again with her father, while Diego was away at the War.

After her terrible experiences during the war, however, she now began to suspect that her knowledge and personality could be enriched by things other than books and reading. Following Diego's death, she had lived through experiences that had undoubtedly changed her: the backbreaking work in the fields, meeting new people, living through cold and tiredness, her encounters with Giulio, her role, no matter how minor, in the Resistance. She had found the resources to manage and organise her own life, to motivate and defend herself. Even her life as a mother was completely different from that she had imagined as a young newly-wed. She saw her son at weekends; she spoke to him without hiding the truth or prevaricating. Gabriele knew his father was dead, he knew his mother had to work to provide for him and he knew how to behave as he should, showing her the proper respect and affection due to her.

Sometimes she thought back to the way she was as a girl and as a young wife, how she had been changed by the cruelties of life. She had no regrets, but instead used these memories to try to understand, to grow, to heal the great sense of dissatisfaction she had. Her feelings of inadequacy perhaps stemmed from her encounter with Giulio and the efforts he made to explain things to her in simple terms. He had talked of many things at length and she had struggled to follow him.

About that time, she found out that the schools were offering evening classes to returning veterans to help them catch up with their studies. These were bound to be somewhat simplified courses because they were aimed at people with jobs and families and therefore with little time to devote to study. She plucked up the courage and, after getting the morning off work, went to the school office to ask about registering. She left with her heart full of hope, having enrolled on a course that would allow her to make up three missed years of her technical schooling and lead on to a diploma in accountancy. She was bursting with joy. She would even be able to afford the second-hand books the school provided with a few small sacrifices.

Her life became frenetic from that day on. She got up early to get to the fields; in the afternoons she would cycle home as fast as she could to study and do her homework. She would be in class from nine in the evening until eleven. When she got home, she had to ignore her tiredness and study for at least another hour. This left her very little time to sleep. She kept the weekends for Gabriele and a little extra rest.

One thing she was sure of was that physical hardships, life in the open air and deprivation had made her stronger, more resilient; able to achieve anything she set her mind to.

Every so often she would see Attilio. Although he was thirty, he was not yet married. Once, Giustina saw him at a fair in Tortoreto with a girl on his arm and was miserable the whole day as a result. It was not because she felt anything more than a fraternal comradeship for him, but because she was alone and his affection for her had been an unfailing point of reference for her in the days of the war. Attilio, realising he had been spotted, had said hello but hadn't managed to hide a certain embarrassment. He had been in love with Giustina for a long time, since Diego had gone off to war. She had probably realised this even then, although she was still too caught up in her pain and too sad to even think about making a new start in life. Now, when he saw her around Giulianova or found some excuse to come up and see her, there was a strained, changed atmosphere around them, of diffidence and lack of trust. Something unresolved lay between them. Giustina never asked, nor did he tell her, about that meeting, or about the girl he was making do with.

One evening, he came round about eight o'clock. Giustina was anxious because she hadn't finished her homework and books and jotters were strewn about her table.

"What on earth are you doing?" he asked, looking at the mess. "Have you started back at school?"

Giustina reddened. This had been her little secret because she was not confident of succeeding and had no desire to broadcast her ambitions in case she did fail in the end.

"What does it look like? I wanted to get my brain moving again. It's gone rusty while my muscles are working all day in the fields. So I've picked up my old schoolbooks. And I'll tell you something: all those things that used to seem so difficult to me, if not completely incomprehensible, are a lot easier now. It's like time and experience have made me better at thinking and understanding."

Attilio looked at her in astonishment. She had changed; she

was speaking in a completely different and more complex way. He could sense how tense she was, however, and made no more of it. Giustina hoped only that he would leave soon because she had to get to school in time for her class.

As soon as he had gone, Giustina leapt on her bicycle and pedalled off quickly towards the village.

In October 1945, Giustina took the oral exam to be admitted into the fifth year of technical school and passed with full marks. The Italian teacher was particularly impressed because she knew some of the most important Italian poets off by heart. She hadn't the courage to tell him that every morning, on the way to the fields, she would recite the most beautiful verses in the anthology to keep herself company. Passing this milestone made her all the more determined to succeed. She expected an even sterner test the following year in the shape of the final examinations. She hoped that a qualification would lead to a better job; perhaps she could keep the books for one of the factories, or be a secretary in the school. Sometimes she thought that, with a bit more preparation, she might be able to work with the local Chamber of Labour to help defend the rights of agricultural labourers, often mistreated and kept as little more than slaves by their bosses.

1946 was a busy year for Giustina. There was a lot for her to read and often she would fall asleep over her open books in the evening. But she was now determined to get her diploma at all costs. During this period she saw Attilio only every once in a while, and only when he came to see her at the house. This was because she was absorbed in her studies, but there was also the fact that he was now engaged to the girl from Tortoreto and she wanted to respect her feelings. Attilio still held a boundless admiration for Giustina, probably hiding deeper feelings, but had found a more normal, less complicated relationship with a simple, affectionate girl. Moreover, with Giustina being admitted to the fifth year of her accountancy night classes, she had reached a higher level of study than he had and this gave him a strange feeling, especially seeing the many books on her shelves that had nothing to do with her exams.

In early July, Giustina sat her exams and got her long-awaited diploma. Her scores for the professional studies side of the examination were nothing to shout about, but her marks for the literary subjects filled her with pride. The head teacher of the school was also the Italian teacher and he complimented her.

"You've done well, Giustina. I've heard that you work as a labourer at the moment, and I hope that this new and well-deserved qualification allows you to find a less strenuous and more satisfying job. You should be very proud of yourself."

Giustina was brought close to tears. She hadn't discussed her studies with anyone, not even her parents, because she didn't want them to worry about her. Now she was sure that she would make them proud. They would have wanted a better future for their daughter than the one that fate had dealt her. Often, her mother thought of the sacrifices she had made to provide for her daughter when she caught sight of her hands, red and coarsened from the work in the fields. On her wedding day her hands had seemed like those of a princess.

As she cycled home, Giustina thought of the results she had achieved, thanks only to her own efforts and determination. She had a job, was better educated and had demonstrated that she could achieve things, if she had something to aim for. She wondered if she would have been able to do these things if Diego were still alive. She realised that in all honesty, her life with Diego would have been very different. She might have had three children by now, and would be devoting all her time to them. Her old schoolbooks would still be stored in a trunk, kept there until the day that her children went off to school. Only then would she have worried about knowing enough to help them study, and would probably have been disappointed.

Even her role as a woman would have been different: Diego was the head of the family, and would have wanted to remain so. He was proud of being able to provide for his family and would never have let his wife go out to work. Wasn't his job good enough? He would eventually have wanted his own business as well: he was an expert mechanic and Antonio still missed him. Even with all these considerations, Giustina always missed him. She was still young, only twenty-seven, and she was all alone.

In spite of the new confidence she had found, she could not bring herself to commit to another relationship, even if she could find someone to love her and take responsibility for Gabriele, because she could not erase Diego from her mind: his abandoned body on the hospital bed, the small wound in his temple. He had sacrificed himself for them, for her and Gabriele. Perhaps he would have died anyway, after months and years of suffering. Perhaps he would have got through it. Who could say?

She knew that Attilio carried a torch for her, a deep affection. But now he had a girl of his own and would be better off creating a family of his own, rather than taking on the family of another man.

Giustina came back to Giulianova after spending the weekend with Gabriele. She had found her son in good spirits; he was six years old now, and was due to start school in the next few days. Sometimes she thought of Gabriele's future and hoped he would be able to study so that he could find a job that was less exhausting than hers. He would be able to read many books and learn many things... like Giulio. She wondered where Giulio was now. Was he still alive? Attilio had told her that the partisan struggle in northern Italy in 1943 was particularly dangerous, but had never spoken of him again.

After Giulio's escape, she had taken the books she and Diego had used at school out of the trunk she kept them in. She was mostly interested in the poetry collections and re-read many old poems. She learned some of them by heart, like "The Dapple-Grey Pony" by Pascoli and "The Infinite" by Leopardi. She read these poems differently now, trying to grasp their true meaning but also, as Giulio would have said, their musicality.

She returned to these books, and many others besides, during these years of study. She particularly liked poetry, but she turned her attention to all forms of literature. She read and reread *The Betrothed* by Manzoni and devoured the whole of Nievo's *Memoirs of an Octogenarian* in a single night.

One afternoon on her way back from work, she noticed a car parked on the gravel road that led to her house. The man leaning against the door of the car began to wave to her. She pedalled faster. As she got closer, she thought she recognised him. It was Giulio! It was really him!

Before she could say anything, she felt his strong arms around her lifting her off the ground. Her face was brought up to his and he kissed her affectionately on both cheeks. "Giustina, Giustina! How happy I am to see you! I'm glad to see you've not changed. Still got your curls, your blue eyes, all those coats and jackets wrapping you up and, praise be! You've still got your black woollen stockings!"

"Giulio, I'm so happy to see you too! I was worried that you hadn't made it!"

"You didn't hear my message?"

"Yes, but then Attilio told me that you had gone up north.

What are you doing here? Why have you come all this way?"

"I'm here to visit you. I had this crazy wish to see you again. Didn't Attilio tell you that I had gone back to Pisa after the war?"

Instead of answering his question, Giustina looked him up and down. Tall, clean-shaven, well dressed; Giulio seemed so different from the man she had hidden in her house three years before.

"You wanted to see me... after three years?" she finally asked.

"Yes. I wanted to wait until you felt better, until your pain had eased with time. It's not been easy... How is Gabriele? I'd like to meet him, if you'll let me."

"Come on inside, Giulio, I have some good red wine and some baking ready."

She opened the door, moving with a newfound spring. She felt Giulio's eyes upon her. He began to look around, and as if bewitched felt all the sensations and impulses of three years ago coming back to him.

"It's just as it was before, Giustina. I'm so happy to see it. But still no books to be found anywhere!" He looked at her with some amusement as he spoke. "I remember looking for something to read one day in the house and all I could find was a missal!"

In answer she slapped him on the arm.

"Ha! Finally... I've pulled the tiger's tail!" he said, laughing.

"If you'd looked harder you'd have found something. My schoolbooks were in the trunk. After you left, I read all those poems again, and I really liked some of them. I didn't really get them when I was a kid. And anyway, I've done a bit of studying in the last couple of years, you know? I've got my diploma now."

"Giustina, that's wonderful! Tell me about it."

He was embarrassed about making fun of her now. He took her hand and held it to his lips. "I'm sorry. I wasn't meaning to criticise. That's how I knew you and that's how I wanted you to stay. I mean to say, you're perfect."

"Where are you staying? Have you got a bed for the night? Did you ask Attilio?"

"I'm staying with him, actually. I've been waiting to come and see you here for three days."

"Well, stay for dinner, then you can head back to his house. I'd be glad of the company; I'm usually all alone."

She shared her meal with Giulio. Later they went to sit on the doorstep and look out into the garden. The kitchen light was on and they could see, here and there in the countryside, the lights of the farmhouses and cottages. The full moon was shining, making the leaves of the trees shimmer.

"See how things have changed! We've come back to life, it's been hard, but we've made it. This is a magical night that I want to remember forever."

"Recite something for me, Giulio. Maybe something by your French poet."

"All right. Here is 'Autumn Song'. It's my favourite of Verlaine's poems.

When a sighing begins
In the violins
Of the autumn-song,
My heart is drowned
In the slow sound
Languorous and long

Pale as with pain,
Breath fails me when
The hour tolls deep.
My thoughts recover
The days that are over
And I weep.

And I go
Where the winds know,
Broken and brief,
To and fro,
As the winds blow
A dead leaf.

"Did you know, Giustina, the Allies used a couple of these lines to warn the French Resistance about the Normandy landings?

Blessent mon coeur
D'une langueur
Monotone.

Giustina hadn't said a word.
"Didn't you like it?"
"It was beautiful, Giulio, beautiful."
She had a lost, far-away look in her eyes. Giulio moved closer and kissed her on the lips. She returned the kiss with equal gentle passion. She was trembling. She had felt nothing like this for a long, long time.
Giulio sat a while in thought, then got up and made ready to leave.
"Are you going?"
"Yes, that would be best. I'll see you tomorrow. When you get back from work, you'll find me here."
She followed him to the door and said goodnight. She had a strange expression on her face, almost absent. He went off with a wave of his hand."
When she came back into the house, Giustina sat down and wrapped her arms around herself. She felt an indefinable sensation, a mixture of extreme happiness and guilt over what

72

seemed to be a betrayal of Diego. She suddenly remembered the pleasure of making love with her husband and began to blush at the thought of her unspoken desire for Giulio, for his lips, for his caresses. She didn't sleep much that night. She rose at dawn to try and calm the nervous tension she had been feeling since Giulio's return.

He was there when she arrived home on her bicycle. She waved at him from way off, smiling. He waited and, when she was close to him, he lifted her up and kissed her. It was not the same kiss as the night before, however. This was a sensual kiss, his tongue entering her mouth.

She did not protest for she had never been kissed like that before. She had wanted that kiss throughout the whole of the night. When they pulled away from each other, she asked him hoarsely, "What do you want, Giulio?"

"You. I've come back for you."

"I can't give myself to anyone," she said, though without conviction.

"You are only twenty-seven. Your life can't be over already. I love you, Giustina, I want you. I've loved you from the first time I saw you bundled up in those daft clothes. Come her, my love. Come to me."

She moved towards him because her will had crumbled.

"Come into the house, I want to undress you. I want to peel the layers off my little onion." He began to remove her coat and her jumper. "How much have you got on?"

He went on undressing her until she stood naked apart from her black woollen stockings, held up by her garters. "Let's leave these on. They've driven me crazy ever since I first set eyes on you."

He stripped quickly and took her with an impetuousness that she had never seen in Diego, even on their honeymoon. He continued to speak even while he moved inside her. "My love, my love. I love you. I've loved you since the moment I saw you. It was so hard for me not to come to you in the night. You were so close to me, and yet so far away. I love you, Giustina. Tell me that you love me."

"Oh, Giulio, Giulio."

"No, tell me you love me. You have to."

"I can't. I can't say it."

"You must find the strength to say it, if it's true. Say it. And tell me that you like me making love to you."

"What sort of person would say a thing like that?"

"All the women I've ever had say it...."

Giustina punched him on the chest as hard as she could, making him jump. He pulled out of her and held her in his arms.

"My little tigress. Tell me you love me, Giustina. Try to say it."

"I ... love you. I love you very much."

He entered her again, and Giustina forgot herself in tiny moans of pleasure.

He came to her house every evening. He was waiting for her when she got back from work, impatient to hold her in his arms. He taught her that love could be expressed in many ways, that feelings could be shouted out and that a woman could take control in a relationship.

"You tell me things I've only heard in films."

"That's because you're a silly curly-headed pumpkin who's afraid of expressing her neuroses."

One evening he took hold of her and pulled her on top of him.

"Now it's your turn to take me."

"What's this all about? You're treating me like a streetwalker!"

"No, I'm treating you like a woman that I love and desire. Gentle now… now move… see, I'm yours."

His hands caressed her full breasts, her tiny waist, her strong hips. Her body was like an hourglass. When she fell, exhausted, at his side, he held her close.

"Come here and tell me you like it."

"I like it."

"You don't waste words, do you?"

"I like it, and I've come back to life with you, Giulio."

"I know, my darling… but think on, I would like to see Gabriele tomorrow."

"Why?"

"Because I have to learn to love him."

She asked him nothing further because his words frightened her.

The next day they went to Tortoreto in the car. Giustina's parents knew Giulio through their daughter's stories, and welcomed him as a friend. Gabriele was at first shy of him, but then began to come to him without fear. He remembered nothing of his dead father, and the affection Giulio showed him touched him. They stayed close together, they held hands, Gabriele asked a thousand questions. Giulio was attentive and loving.

On their way back to Giulianova, Giustina asked Giulio, "Why did you want to see Gabriele? Why did you do it?"

"Let me answer you with a question, Giustina. Why do you think I came back here?"

"I don't know. To see me, perhaps. I was the girl you… never managed to… have."

"That's unkind. I came back because I want to marry you, because I want you to be my wife, my little savage wife, and because I want Gabriele to have a father, to study, to go to university and to be somebody."

She looked at him with a strange light in her eyes.

"I don't want to rush you, Giustina, because I know you didn't expect this from me. Don't judge me for less than I am. I like to have you, to love you, to hold you in my arms. But I also want you to be the mother of my children, Gabriele's brothers and sisters, and want us to be finally able to find a bit of peace and happiness. In a few days I have to go back to Pisa, where my students are waiting for their exams. Can you give me an answer before I leave? I must tell you that I'm persistent, especially when the stakes are high..."

"I'm a high stake for you?"

"The very highest. You're a real woman, sincere, unblemished, quintessential. And where can I find a worse-dressed woman... I ask you? I'm not a big one for fashion. It was those black stockings that did for me."

They got out of the car and he stayed with her the whole night. He let her sleep on when dawn came.

They saw each other the next day but Giulio did not renew his request. Instead he watched her, his eyes intense, hoping she would appreciate and feel his anxiety.

But Giustina was living her own dilemma. On the one hand there was Giulio, a new marriage, a secure future, a different life for her and for Gabriele, who could at last have a father. She was suffering for his sake for she knew that her son's future depended on her choice. He could study, go to university, become a professional or even a professor. She was sure of Giulio's love and tenderness after years apart. She was not likely to have a rush of blood to the head at her age: she was sure his intentions were honest.

On the other hand there was Diego. There was the memory of Diego, his awful death, of which Giulio could know nothing. After all these years, she could never forget his desperate expression in death and the choice he had made for her and Gabriele. She felt that with that action, he had tied them to himself forever.

She didn't want to discuss the issue with Giulio right here and now. When she saw him, she threw her arms around his neck uninhibitedly and said to him, "I've thought a lot about your proposal, Giulio, and I keep coming back to how different our social worlds are. I can't help thinking that I must answer you in this way: aren't we fine as we are? Why do we have to change our lives with a wedding? Is my love not enough for you?"

Giulio looked at her somewhat impatiently, then calmly said, "Your love means a lot to me, Giustina, but after so many hardships and setbacks, I want a family of my own and children with you. Why should we live with an inconvenient arrangement when you and I are both free? You're hesitating because your husband died in the war, but how many war widows remarry? You're young and you have your whole life in front of you. Gabriele deserves a family. I'll do anything to make you happy."

Giustina fell silent, knowing that everything Giulio had said was perfectly logical. But Diego had killed himself for that war pension. It wasn't enough, in truth, but he had killed himself. If she remarried, she would with one action, one single action, render his sacrifice in vain.

That night she couldn't sleep. The problem would remain in their lives as long as they continued to see each other. She was tormented by a million questions, a million doubts, but she had no one to confide in. She kept crying and the following morning her eyes were puffy and red.

Giulio sensed all of this and it made him feel as though he would die. He knew that Giustina was suffering, but could not understand why. He had fallen in love with her almost at once. He had been attracted by her dignified suffering, by her lack of coquettishness despite her beauty and by her simple way of treating people. Behind all that, however, he had immediately perceived her femininity, her uncommon sensuality and sensitivity. It was there, even in the way she moved. Loving her, he found that she was sensual and passionate in a way he had never experienced in any other woman. Now he wanted her, desired only her, needed her to be his life's companion. What was stopping her? Had she loved her husband so much that she could not forget him or ever put another man in his place? What was her relationship with her first love like? Giulio felt something close to jealousy as he considered these questions. He recognised this and worried that Diego was fated always to come between them.

The days passed and Giustina could not come to a decision. She would nestle herself in his arms yet never seem quite happy. She came to him at night and loved him with a passion and intensity that gave him a sense of how great her love was for him. So why hesitate, then?

Now he had to leave, and Giustina had no time left for indecision.

"I have to go back to Pisa tomorrow. I can't stay any longer. You've not given me an answer, so I have to assume that you have no intention of accepting my proposal. I'm sorry about this, because I had hoped that my wandering days were over and that you would have made a home with me. My love for you is boundless, but I cannot wait forever..."

Giustina seemed driven to desperation. She held him close to her as she tried to find the courage to express her feelings directly.

"I love you, Giulio, I've never loved anyone like I love you.

I love you and desire you, because being with you makes me feel better than you can imagine. I like everything about you; don't leave me, please. Love me as I am, without ties. If you want, I'll come to Pisa with you. I'll live in your house with Gabriele. We'll love each other all the same and I'll care for the children that our love brings."

Giulio was taken aback. He had not expected that a girl from a little village, bound by the social conventions that had conditioned her life and choices, could have made such a suggestion. But he replied firmly, "No, I can't have that. I can't, out of respect for you. I'm looking for a woman who will be mine always, to be the mother of my children in every way. If I take that advantage of you, without tying you to me somehow, I'd feel guilty.

"What would we tell our children? That we didn't marry because we didn't love each other enough? And who would I be to Gabriele? His mother's lover? How would I introduce you to my family and my colleagues at the University? No, Giustina, I can't accept. I want your respect, Gabriele's respect and the respect of our future children. I have to be an example, and not in a position of weakness.

At this point, Giustina began to cry. She sobbed and wrung her hands. Giulio could not make any sense of this show of desperation. He didn't understand.

"Don't cry, my darling. I won't ask any more of you. I will leave tomorrow and if you want to see me again, you can contact me. Call me, write to me. I just want to say that I don't understand you."

Giustina looked at him through her tears. He was handsome, still young, rich and in love with her. He was everything a woman could want, but he was not for her.

She managed to find the strength to tell him the truth. "Giulio, I'm dying inside. Believe me. I love you so much… I don't want to live without you. But I can't give up the war pension… because … Diego killed himself so that Gabriele and I could have it."

She was sobbing, and now that she had said it, she covered her face with her hands.

"What!" Giulio exclaimed.

"Yes, when I got to the hospital in Torre Annuziata, Diego had just shot himself. He had written a note to explain why he had done it. Now do you understand? If I married you, it would be making his death meaningless. He killed himself… he shot himself." She was shouting now. Giulio held her and tried to calm her, rocking her gently.

"Yes, darling, now I understand. Even though it doesn't change things. I'm leaving tomorrow, and if you still want me – under my conditions – you can let me know."

He left her that evening when he saw she had finally calmed down. He kissed her for a long time and held her to his chest.

"Goodbye, Giustina. Remember that I have loved you for years. My address and telephone number are on the table."

He left quickly and got into the car, starting the engine. Giustina was at the door, watching him leave. What madness was this? She was only twenty-seven and had given up on life.

She threw herself onto her bed and cried for the whole of the night.

In the early morning, she got up to go to work, trying hard not to think. It was over, because she had wanted it to be over. He had said, "If you want you can call me", but what was she supposed to say?

While she pedalled sadly towards the countryside, she was thinking, "If he really loves me, he'll never give up on me. He waited for three years before, and he might come round to my point of view. Would it matter if our children were illegitimate? What does it matter if we love each other?" She was unsure of the things going through her mind, and deep down she hoped above all else that the love Giulio had for her, a love above all others, was real, and not just a figment of her imagination. She knew he was a real man and would never settle for living in the invidious state she had proposed, when it would be just as easy to make it legal.

She reached the field and took up her basket for collecting grapes. Her eyes were red with tears and lack of sleep. The thought of Giulio would not leave her. She called out to him in her heart and begged him to come back.

"Maybe in time, maybe he'll understand… and he'll come running back to me," she thought, tears coursing down her cheeks.

But would he?

A fortnight passed without a letter, postcard or even so much as a sign of interest from Pisa. Giustina was distressed and confused. She had taken a decision – or rather not taken a decision – that had surprised then disappointed Giulio. He had been sure that his proposal would be accepted joyfully. Now she wasn't so sure, tormented with worries and regrets. She was very much in love with him and she had for him such feelings as she had never known in her life.

Although Giulio had said in parting that he wouldn't come looking for her again, she continued to hope for some sign from him that he too was suffering from being so far away from her.

She continued to work in the fields, but as winter approached, she put word around that she was looking for other work, in the hope of finding something less strenuous. The head of the school where she had studied had given her a reference for a job at the post office in the village and she anxiously waited news about the position. A consistent, reliable wage – even if it weren't much, in truth – would give her a far better life and allow her to think of Gabriele's continuing education. The boy was showing a passionate interest in his schooling.

While she was in the village shopping one Saturday afternoon, she met Attilio.

"We hardly ever see you round here nowadays! I hear there might be a job for you at the post office."

Giustina smiled. "Says who? I've applied, but I haven't heard anything. I'd be a happy woman if it were true."

They walked along together in silence, side by side. Then Attilio said, "What did you say to Giulio to make him run off like that? I've not heard from him in a month, and he usually sends a card or something."

Giustina reddened and asked in a low voice, "What makes you think I had anything to do with it? What am I to him?"

Attilio stopped and looked her in the eye. "Didn't he come back for you? Isn't he in love with you? Where was he all those nights he didn't come back to my place? Wasn't he sleeping with you? His car was always parked at your door…"

She reddened again and her answer revealed her annoyance. "You and I are friends, but I won't let you interfere in my private life. Where Giulio might have slept, I have no idea. He knows lots of people in this area. As for his car, are you saying that you were spying on me? Remember that he's a university professor and I'm just a peasant. What could we have in common?"

"You might have nothing in common. He was in love with you none the less," was Attilio's confident reply.

"What's it to you, even if it were true?"

"I'm in love with you too, and have been, ever since Diego went off to Africa – as I'm sure you know."

Giustina's look showed her irritation.

"You're so in love with me that you've been seeing a young thing in Tortoreto for the past two years. I've been hearing that she's pregnant. Congratulations! What do you want with me, anyway? What's keeping you from marrying her? All I can say is that if you wanted to ruin our friendship, you've certainly done a fine job!" Saying this, she turned her back on him and walked away.

The next morning she cycled over to see Gabriele at Tortoreto. He ran to her and hugged her tight.

"When can I come and live with you, mamma? I'm a big boy now. You can leave me at home and I won't cause any problems."

Giustina stroked his head and looked at him lovingly.

"If I can get a job that means I'm only away from home while you're at school, I'll move you in straight away. But you must be patient for a little while more." They spent the day talking about everything that had happened during the week.

Gabriele was doing well at school; he was the best in his class. He loved studying and always asked for books as presents. He read a lot and, importantly, remembered what he had read. Giustina warned him gently, "If you go on like this, you'll need glasses before you're twenty."

"Oh, I'm not bothered about that, mamma. I just like reading about things. When I grow up I want to be an engineer that designs planes. Planes that go faster than sound. And see-through submarines that go down to the bottom of the sea to look at plants. Do you think I can?"

His mother looked at him with some concern. "Well, we don't always get what we wish for. Have you thought about a more practical job?"

Gabriele seemed worried. "I like thinking about dad, though I never knew him except through your stories. But I don't think I'd like to be a mechanic. I don't really like motorbikes."

Giustina brought the conversation to a close; it was too soon to be thinking about Gabriele's future, especially because she herself had not yet found a better job than that of a farm hand. Gabriele's dream would have meant moving to a university town like Rome, Bologna or Padua.

A month later, Giustina got a call from the village post office. When she heard the message she could not hold back the tears. She would now earn a regular wage, one that was higher that she had hoped for, and her life would now be simpler and more normal, without as much physical hardship.

Because her work kept her busy also in the afternoons, she could not have Gabriele to stay with her just yet. He would have too much time alone after leaving school for that to be feasible. He'd have to wait until he was a bit older.

There were about ten other people working in the post office, of whom four were women. The boss was a kind and approachable man called Mario Ferretti; he was known in the village as a man of integrity. Giustina met him one evening after work as he was walking with his wife and three sons. He stopped to introduce his wife, praising his new employee's resourcefulness and precision, her reserve and brightness. Giustina felt embarrassed as his wife scrutinised her with some curiosity. Like everyone else in the village, she knew that Giustina was a war widow who had fought with the partisans, and some said she had taken a liking to a stranger she had got to know at that time.

Giustina looked back at Signora Ferretti. She was pleasant, plump, around forty, with an ample bust. She was known for her wifely and motherly virtues. The boys were handsome young men between the ages of fourteen and seventeen. They looked like their father, especially in the reddish tint of their hair and their clear green eyes.

At lunchtime, Giustina would leave the office to eat a sandwich that she had brought from home. Sometimes she would be alone, and sometimes she would be with colleagues who also came from outside the village. Sometimes, Signor Ferretti would be there as well.

He was a pleasant man, witty and sensitive to his charges in his conversation, and not particularly focused on the women in the office. However, Giustina noticed that his gaze frequently followed her around and lingered on her hips and legs, legs that were now covered by silk rather than woollen stockings. Her clothes had changed now that she was putting as much care into her appearance as she had when she was a girl.

One late afternoon, she had found herself alone in the office with her boss, finishing the last of the day's formalities. He had come close to her and asked in a gentle voice, "Don't you feel lonely, Giustina? You're young, and you must sometimes think of love, especially as you have known it before."

Giustina had blushed, rushed to finish the last of the paperwork and headed for the door, saying, "I don't so much as let it cross my mind, sir. I have a child to bring up and I don't have the time for such distractions." She had hurried away in order not to prolong the embarrassing scene.

Attilio was at the junction that led to her house. He seemed to be waiting for her. She hadn't seen him for more than two months and decided to act as if there had been no argument between them. She got off her bicycle and spoke to him warmly. "Were you waiting for me, Attilio? Did you hear I have a job at the post office now? It's a lot less tiring! How are things with you?"

"Yes, I heard about the job. I'm glad to hear you're not killing yourself with the work out in the countryside. I'm doing fine… Look, I wanted to tell you that… I'm getting married on Saturday. Delia is pregnant and there's nothing else I can do. I would really have liked to marry you and take care of Gabriele, who is, after all, the son of my best friend. But life doesn't always go the way we plan."

"It's a little late for regrets now. Anyway, I told you that I have no interest in remarrying anyone."

"Why, Giustina? You're young; it's a real pity that a special girl like you could be alone for the rest of her life. Even if I can't have you, I wish you would think it over. I'm sure Diego wouldn't have wanted you to be all alone and... defenceless... so to speak."

They both laughed at this last suggestion. Then Attilio told her, "I can't invite you to the wedding, Giustina. I don't like saying this. It's just that... Delia is so jealous... She might cause a scene."

"Jealous of me? Why?"

"She thinks that there might have been something between us during the Occupation."

"Well, there wasn't, so you can tell her to rest easy. For my part, I'll be happy to stay away from the church on Saturday."

They said goodbye and Giustina carried on towards the house.

There were several envelopes and advertisements in her letterbox. Immediately she spotted one bearing Giulio's precise and even handwriting. She felt her heart beat more strongly and faster. She went inside, sat at the table and held the envelope in her hand for a few minutes, asking herself what could be inside. Had he written to say that he had thought things over and was coming back? Or was he announcing that he was engaged to another woman after her prolonged silence?

She opened the letter with trembling hands and read:

My dearest, darling Giustina,

I am writing to you to say that, since our parting, I have been thinking over and over again about Diego's passing and his desperate decision. And I have been thinking about how sad it must have been and how sad it must be for you. It must have seemed so unjust. I have, as I promised, not sought you out, because I have no desire to torment you with what must seem like my obsessive love. But I would like you to reflect on something, which is this: If Diego had got to the point of coughing up blood, there was no longer any hope for him. In those days there was no cure, and even now I doubt that antibiotics would help much in such an advanced stage of tuberculosis. Diego probably worked this out, and this was cause of the deep depression in him that brought him to his early death. He wanted to give you an explanation for this – *not* to bind you to him forever, but to justify his action. If he had died naturally, which he probably would have within a couple of weeks, you would still have had his war pension.

If you decide to start living again, not necessarily with me, please remember that, even though you will lose the pension, you will still have your son. I'm sorry if I sound rather brutal, but I want to make you think, to reflect.

I send you all my love.

Giulio.

After reading the letter, Giustina brought it to her lips, and then to her cheek. "He hasn't forgotten me," she thought, "he hasn't betrayed my love. I'm still in his heart." She burst into tears. She had already thought of things exactly as Giulio had written. Knowing Diego, he had surely not intended to tie her to him with that terrible act. Probably he was, as Giulio suggested, completely destroyed and desperate. The idea of living as he was, even for a few weeks, must have terrified him.

Yet she continued to hesitate. In those two months since Giulio had left she had thought about him every moment of every day. She remembered the love and passion that had brought them into each other's arms.

She had also tried to imagine her life as a simple country girl beside a university professor. She was sure that, in the end, he would tire of her and be ashamed of her clumsiness. This conviction persisted despite the fact that that side of her character had always seemed to please him, and he had spoken of her as a wife and as the future mother of his children.

She wiped her eyes and drove away the thoughts of a future that was surely impossible now. Her daily reality now was simpler and more normal: she had a decent job and a good place to work… except that her boss was now trying to court her, albeit in a furtive way. He surely thought, like many others, that a young widow, with experience of the matrimonial bed and knowledge of the opposite sex, would be fair game. She forced him from her thoughts for the rest of the day and the days that followed, avoiding being left alone with him.

She managed this for a few weeks until one afternoon he asked her to stay behind with him to finish an important stock check. They ended up alone together, but there was a definite tension in the air. Giustina was on her guard, and watched him out of the corner of her eye. They worked away for a good half hour before Ferretti said, "Let's take a break, Giustina, my head's bursting."

They stopped and looked each other in the eye. Giustina did not like what she saw and got up to pick up another file to try to distract him. In an instant he was on her. He pushed her up against the wall with a strength that Giustina couldn't believe. He pushed his erection against her and, holding her arms, moved his mouth close to hers.

"You feel it? Remember it? You love it, don't you? You're

gorgeous. That feline body of yours… I get such a thrill just seeing you walk."

She tried to scream, but his mouth was on hers now, his tongue penetrating her, almost suffocating her. He continued to press himself against her. She finally managed to push him off, running to the door and out of the office. She had left her purse and keys, but did not feel safe enough to go back in alone. At that moment, she saw Silvana walking along the pavement and called out to her. Her sister-in-law was surprised to see her, dishevelled and still in her black work apron.

"What's happened to you?" she asked, frightened.

"Please, just come in with me till I get my purse. That pig of a boss is trying to molest me."

Silvana looked at her perplexed, but agreed to do so. When they entered the office, everything seemed normal. Ferretti sat there smoking a cigarette. The paperwork that had been knocked over had been re-ordered on the desk. Giustina picked up her purse, took off her apron and left without saying a word.

"Now will you tell me what happened? What did he want?"

Giustina burst into tears. "The bastard kissed me and rubbed himself up against me like a dog on heat. What am I supposed to do? I have to work there…"

Silvana linked her arm with Giustina's and said: "I'm going to walk you home because I must have a serious talk with you. My dearest little brother has been dead now for a long time. I miss him every day. But you don't seem to want anything from life other than to remember his death. You're young, Giustina. You must think about having a family again, about finding a man who will give you and Gabriele the chance to be part of a family. I hoped you might marry Attilio, whom I've known since he was a boy, but he's taken now. You want to be like me? I've been engaged for twenty years, waiting for Alfredo to marry me. We'll never be together if he continues like this and, even if we were to marry, I'll be very lucky to have children at forty. Please don't throw your life away. You're like a lamb amongst so many wolves, a young, beautiful widow like you. What that pig did to you shows how desirable you still are. You're young, Giustina, you can still find love and have children, being as beautiful as you are."

The two women embraced and Giustina wept out her humiliation on Silvana's shoulder.

Back in the house, Giustina thought over what had happened in the office and what Silvana had said to her. She had barely mentioned the war pension or Diego's death. Years had passed. She was young and had to think differently about her life and the life of her son.

"Perhaps you will find a new love," Silvana had said.

But she already had one.

The next day, after work, she went to the station to ask which train she should catch to get to Pisa from Giulianova. The clerk was very helpful. She could get a train to Ancona and from there reach Pisa by way of Bologna and Florence. The ticket wouldn't be too expensive.

Giulio hadn't been in touch for several months now, and she hadn't so much as sent him a postcard either. What would be the upshot of her turning up unannounced in Pisa? She wondered if he had promised to wait for her sincerely, or as a ruse to get her to accept his proposal. She could have written to him and he would presumably have come running to her, but she was convinced that they would have to look into each others' eyes before coming to a decision, after so long apart.

She had no experience of travelling: the only time she had been away from Giulianova and Tortoreto was to visit Diego in the military hospital at Torre Annuziata. Even on that occasion she had been with the far more practically-minded Silvana. She was older now, and more experienced, and would not get lost. She would follow the instructions the railway clerk gave her.

A couple of days later she asked for a holiday from work, citing family business as her reason, and got ready to leave. She put a couple of changes of clothes in a suitcase and decided not to tell anyone, not even her parents, what she intended doing. Following her instructions, she got to Ancona, then on to Bologna and Florence, before arriving in Pisa in the late afternoon.

Near the station she found a cheap little hotel, changed her clothes and left her suitcase. She asked for directions to the street that Giulio lived on, and soon found herself standing nervously across the street from his front door, wondering how to tackle the situation.

It was nearly seven o'clock in the evening now, and Giulio was still not home: his car, which she knew well, was nowhere to be seen. The best solution, then, would be to wait for his arrival and then surprise him.

She hadn't long to wait: about twenty minutes later, Giulio's car pulled up in front of the house. She waited for a moment before crossing the road because she immediately sensed that he wasn't alone.

Giulio got out of the car and went around to the passenger side to open the door for a smiling young woman. She got out and they stopped to talk. He leant against the car and smoothed her hair that had been ruffled by the wind. They kept talking and laughing, and he kept on touching her hair.

They talked for at least half an hour. They finally embraced and Giulio held the woman's head against his shoulder, pressing his lips against her. They said goodbye and she went off round the corner of the building.

Giustina could not control her fury. Before her stood a man who had sworn he was completely lost in love for her, ready to wait forever for her, a man who seconds ago was in the arms of some young thing, shameless and unthinking. Of course Giulio could wait for her forever, because in the meantime he could spend the time dallying with some student or other. There was a moment's hesitation while Giulio, after retrieving his briefcase and some papers from his car, stopped to light a cigarette.

She made her decision. She had travelled hundreds of miles to see him and now had to tell him exactly what she thought of him, there, in the middle of the street, with all these people watching. Perhaps they even knew him.

She had just reached the other side of the street when he saw her. There was a moment of incredulity and disbelief before a wide smile lit up his face. He recognised her despite her new clothes, despite her looking different from any other occasion he had seen her. He walked towards her with arms open wide, saying, "Giustina! My love! You're finally here! Or am I dreaming?"

Giustina hit him full in the face with her handbag. It was quite heavy, and he staggered backwards. She started shouting, regardless of the curious passers-by.

"You rotten pig! 'My love'? My arse. You two-faced liar, I saw you with that hussy…"

She lifted up her bag again and he just managed to grab her wrist to stop the blow.

"Woaaah, Giustina, calm down! That hussy is my niece, Elisa. Paola's daughter. My sister, Paola!"

She stopped and looked at him in astonishment.

"Do you hug all your nieces like that?" she said in a barely audible voice.

"Well… yes. Especially because today my eldest niece had her first exam at the University. She was so happy."

Giustina lowered her eyes and said simply, "Sorry…"

He took her by the arm and said, in a sad voice, "Come on, let's go to a bar. I need a cognac, and you need a camomile tea. I'll need to get some ice because I think my eyelid is swelling up."

She finally looked up at his face and almost cried out when she saw him. His eye had all but disappeared under the swelling.

"Oh, my god, Giulio, I'm so very sorry."

They reached the café and sat at a little table in a corner. They ordered a cognac and a camomile tea. The waiter, who knew Giulio, asked him what had happened to his eye.

"I caught it against the car door. Could you give me a bit of ice, please?"

The waiter ran off and Giustina sat in front of Giulio, eyes lowered.

"I'm sorry, Giulio. I came all the way to Pisa full of hope for our future… and now look what I've done…"

"You didn't even give me chance to explain… you're still a little tiger, a wildcat…"

The waiter came back with a napkin full of ice and Giulio held it to his temple and over his eye. Giustina looked at him, cowed.

"How can I make this up to you? It's just that I'm a jealous woman and … well, I love you… you do know that, don't you?"

"If I'd wanted to mess around here in Pisa, why would I have kept on declaring my love for you? You were so far away, I could have just stopped chasing after you."

"That's true enough. But I'm still a jealous woman and, if you betray me, I'll be only too happy… and able… to give you such a smack…"

He stopped her, placing a hand on her arm, pressing down upon it.

"So... you're still making threats... Well, just remember that I went through paratrooper training and fought with the partisans... I could kill you with a single blow."

Giustina blinked. "Are you serious?"

He burst out laughing. "No, not at all... I want to treat you with endless sweetness for the rest of your life... Let's go back to my place so we can discuss our future."

"I left my suitcase at a hotel near the station."

"We'll get it tomorrow... You'll do fine as you are this evening, and we won't need any nightwear..."

He paid the bill and they walked out arm in arm.

Giulio's house left Giustina speechless. It had massive rooms, antique cabinets full of silver objects, Murano glass lampshades. The nicest room was Giulio's bedroom. It was big, with a comfortable bed, a huge wardrobe with inset mirrors and a bathroom ensuite.

Thoughts were galloping through Giustina's brain. He had a house like this, and yet he had come after her, a woman – no longer as young as she once was – with a son, no education to compare with his, from a little village in Abruzzo... A question came to her lips: "Why me?"

He took her in his arms and kissed her before answering.

"Because I fell in love with you. Is that a good enough answer?"

"But what did you see in me?"

"You're beautiful, you have lovely soft curly hair that I love to touch. You have a well-proportioned body, with that little waist and those fine hips that have me contemplating several happy future children. Now come here, I want to adore you utterly. You'll just have to excuse me..."

They stripped naked and gave themselves up to their every desire.

After making love, they lay side by side. Giustina asked, her voice a little concerned, "But do you know why I came to Pisa?"

"I hope it wasn't just to smack my face. Seeing as you are still here, though, I assume you will be accepting my proposal of marriage..."

She thought a while, then said, "Are you still sure you want to marry me?"

He hugged her. "More than ever. With you, I am happy. You just have to decide where you want to marry me. Here in Pisa, in Tortoreto, in Giulianova… If you want I can convert to Buddhism, Islam, Protestantism…"

"Why go to all that trouble? The church in Giulianova with a few family members will do me fine. My parents are too old now to travel far."

They held each other in silence for a while before Giustina dared to tell him of her conditions.

"There is something I have to tell you, Giulio. Maybe you won't understand, and won't want to marry me anymore."

"What's happened, my darling?" he asked, apprehensively.

"If I marry you, I give up Diego's pension, but I can't and won't give up my job at the post office. I worked so hard to get it."

"Is that *it*?" he asked, "You can get a transfer to Pisa for family reasons, and I will do my best to get it all arranged quickly."

"But I'll have to go back to Giulianova next week."

"Ok, I'll go with you. I can get a few days off and we can publish our banns. How's that? Remember, I won't have you facing your problems alone anymore. We shall have to prepare Gabriele for his life with a new family in a new town... Your parents as well..."

"There's something else as well, Giulio…"

"Oh no... There's more?"

"I don't want to sell my house in Giulianova because… well,

it's my house, the only one I've ever had and it cost me all of my savings…"

Giulio thought for a moment, then said, "We won't sell it. We'll use it as a summer house. We'll need to add an extension to get the two or three extra rooms that we we'll need for Gabriele and the others when they arrive… Any more problems, Giustina?"

"No," she said, "now I'm quite contented."

The next morning Giulio went to collect Giustina's suitcase from her hotel. When he returned later that day, he asked her to dress up a bit. She was surprised.

"Why? Where are we going?"

"Today, I want you to meet my family. My father passed away during the war, but my mother, my brother and my two sisters can't wait to meet you. I, for my part, want things sewn up before you can change your mind."

"You won't be ashamed of me?"

"I will be very proud of you."

They set out in the late afternoon. They hadn't far to walk; Giulio's mother lived a few streets away.

They entered a luxurious room, and Giustina was greeted with a confusion of faces; several people were looking at her, among them a grand old lady with white hair, and a little girl of eight or nine. Everyone's attention was fixed upon her. Giulio took her by the arm and proudly introduced her to his mother.

"This is Giustina. I have finally persuaded her to marry me."

Giustina blushed and lowered her eyes.

Giulio's mother broke the silence. "At long last! We get to meet the famous Giustina!" Saying this, she looked at her son and asked in a worried voice, "But what's happened to your eye, Giulio?"

"I banged into my car door, mamma. It's nothing." Giustina reacted immediately. She approached the old lady and crouched down at her feet, taking her hand.

"It wasn't his car door, Signora Malinverni. I hit him with my handbag."

"You... did that, Giustina?"

"Yes. I did." Her face was thoroughly red now with the shame and confusion.

Giulio thought it best to clarify the situation. "She saw me giving Elisa a hug and thought I had another girlfriend."

Everyone laughed at once and only then did Giustina dare to lift her eyes to her future mother-in-law, smiling apologetically. The old lady stroked her hair, reassuring her.

"Get up, my dear girl, and come and sit beside me. What lovely hair you have! And such pretty eyes! Giulio was right to persevere and... between you and me, it's a good idea to keep 'em in check every once in a while..."

Giulio introduced her to the family, to Paola, his elder sister, her husband and their daughter Elisa who hugged her affectionately. She met his brother, who was the father of the little girl who was the same age as Gabriele, and finally, his younger sister.

The little girl asked about her new cousin. "When will you bring Gabriele to see us? I've been waiting... oh, ever since I left nursery."

Giustina put her arms round her and said, speaking so everyone present could hear, "Gabriele will be very happy to come and see you. He will be as happy as I am... happier than I could ever have hoped to be after so much sadness."